COUNT RODERIC'S CASTLE

COUNT RODERIC's
C A S T L E :

OR,

GOTHIC TIMES,

A TALE.

━━━━━━

In winter's tedious nights, sit by the fire,
With good old folks, and let them tell thee tales
Of woeful ages long ago betide.

SHAK. RICH. II.

━━━━━━

WITH A NEW INTRODUCTION BY
HANNAH DOHERTY HUDSON

VALANCOURT BOOKS

First published London: William Lane, 1794
First Valancourt Books edition 2017

This edition © 2017 by Valancourt Books
Introduction © 2017 by Hannah Doherty Hudson

Published by Valancourt Books, Richmond, Virginia
http://www.valancourtbooks.com

All Valancourt Books publications are printed on acid free paper
that meets all ANSI standards for archival quality paper.

ISBN 978-1-943910-59-5
Also available as an electronic book.

Set in Dante MT

CONTENTS

INTRODUCTION

WRITING in 1793, an irritable contributor to the *English Review* complained that "As the quantity of novels with which Mr Lane deluges the public is very large, it must be expected that some of them will be indifferent ... the incidents have been so often repeated that they not only cease to please, but begin almost to disgust" (306). The novel that inspired this critique was *Mortimore Castle*, published by William Lane's Minerva Press. Only founded in 1790, the Press had nonetheless rapidly established itself in the publishing world, edging out older and more respectable competitors with vast numbers of novels, an in-house circulating library, and a host of savvy marketing strategies.[1] The fashion with which the Minerva Press was soon most associated was the new passion for gothic novels. Following upon Horace Walpole's influential *The Castle of Otranto* (1764) and, more recently, the breakthrough success of Ann Radcliffe's second novel, *The Romance of the Forest* (1791), readers sought more thrilling tales of terror set in distant lands and times long past.[2] While numerous presses published such novels, it was Lane, as the *English Review* writer suggests, who did so with such volume that the reputation of the gothic genre itself would soon be tied up with the reputation of his press. The rapid rise of the novel in the late eighteenth century was thus also the rise of the Minerva Press and the rise of the gothic.[3] Of the 655 novels published by London publishers

[1] See Raven 79-80 for a concise discussion of Lane's Minerva Press: for more extended, if older, accounts of the Press, see Blakey and McLeod.

[2] St. Clair (631) gives statistics on Radcliffe's book sales; for more on Radcliffe's life and works, see Norton, *Mistress of Udolpho*, and Miles, *Ann Radcliffe*.

[3] Raven's Introduction to *The English Novel*, vol. I, provides the most reliable statistics on the increasing numbers of novels produced in England in the last decades of the eighteenth century. While my own introduction is by no means a compre-

viii INTRODUCTION

in the 1790s, fully 217 of them were published by Lane, more
than four times as many as any other publisher.[1] While many
of these works were not gothic novels at all, enough of them
were that the connection between publisher and genre was
firmly established in the public imagination. The reviewer's
critique of *Mortimore Castle* was thus not directed solely at
the work itself, but also at the "quantity of novels" produced
by Lane, with their "incidents … so often repeated." Gothic
settings too made easy targets, as the castle-heavy titles of
this period make plain.[2] *Mortimore Castle* was just one of several novels in 1793 to prominently include "Castle" on their
title-page, and the trend showed no signs of abating: in 1794,
the novel newly republished in this volume, *Count Roderic's
Castle: or, Gothic Times, a Tale* was one of six titles—more
than ten percent of all the novels published that year—to
follow in Horace Walpole's titular footsteps.[3] The Minerva
Press accounted for five of these, counting *Castle Zittaw* and
The Haunted Castle among its 1794 offerings. *Count Roderic's
Castle*, then, though a new novel, was in many ways received
and reviewed as a known commodity, one more entry in an
already well-defined (and to some observers, already over-
saturated) category.[4] The impression of similarity is height-

---

hensive overview of scholarship on the eighteenth-century Gothic novel, a number of influential scholars are cited in the notes below; in addition to these, a few
additional works are worthy of note. For early scholarship on the popular gothic,
see especially Birkhead, Summers, and Tompkins. Among the more recent works
of scholarship that I have found particularly influential are Miles, *Gothic Writing*,
Lynch, Sedgwick, Ellis, Watt and Gamer.

1 Raven 73. This count includes a few novels which were published by the author
but printed by Lane at the Minerva Press. Given that these works were still published with the distinctive Minerva logo on the title page, I've included them here
within the group of books that would have been imaginatively associated with
the Minerva brand.

2 See Moretti and Jockers 56 for discussion of eighteenth-century titling trends,
and "castle" in titles in particular.

3 Based on Garside et al.'s count of 56 novels for 1794 (Vol. I., 601-628).

4 Of course, as I will argue is the case for *Count Roderic's Castle*, the castles in
these novels are even more crucial to the plot than to the title: Punter refers to
"the angry and potent ruins from which the first Gothic novelists built their literary dreams and nightmares" (4), while Botting calls the castle "[t]he major locus

ened both by the novel's genre-evocative title (in addition to "castle," "count" and "gothic" are also clearly designed to trigger readerly recognition)[1] and by the absence of other indications of provenance: the novel, like many others of the era, was published anonymously, and nothing of the author is currently known.[2]

At a mere two volumes, *Count Roderic's Castle* is a brief novel, especially by comparison to other well-known gothic works such as Ann Radcliffe's *Mysteries of Udolpho*, published in the same year in four volumes, each in excess of 400 pages. However, it is by no means uneventful. The novel is set in an undefined, quasi-medieval-era Italy, "In those days when Astolpho, surnamed the Proud, beheld his regal sway extended over the rich and fertile plains of Lombardy," and revolves around two closely interconnected plots. The first focuses on the love affairs of three young noblemen, Count Rhinaldo, Count Tancred, and Count Anselmo, and their beloveds, Isabel, Aspasia, and Ellenor, respectively. While the mutual affection of each young pair is never in doubt, their happiness is repeatedly thwarted by the machinations of their antagonists, King Astolpho, his friend Count St. Amand, and St. Amand's son Rhodolpho, who abduct, imprison, and imperil the ladies for various personal and political reasons. The second plot centers on the battle

of Gothic plots," arguing that "Architecture ... signalled the spatial and temporal separation of the past and its values from those of the present" (2-3). On the Minerva Press novel as "dependable commodity," see Clery, *Rise of Supernatural Fiction*, esp. 136-7.

1 See Miles, "The 1790s: The Effulgence of the Gothic" on the "marketing cues" of the 1790s gothic genre (41). Note, however, Clery's assertion in her essay in the same volume, "The Genesis of 'Gothic' Fiction," that "[t]he 'Gothic novel' is thus mostly a twentieth-century coinage" (21). Clery cites a few other novels with "Gothic" in the title (not mentioning *Count Roderic's Castle*) but makes the point that, while readers at the time certainly noted generic similarities between many of these novels, they would have been much more likely to identify them as "romances" than as "gothic novels."

2 Raven notes that "over 80 per cent of all novel titles in the 1770s and 1780s were published anonymously," with the numbers falling only somewhat in the 1790s (41).

for the throne of Lombardy, and features the three young heroes plotting, and then fighting, to overthrow Astolpho, whom they deem a usurper, in order to replace him with the rightful king. Coincidences abound as the two plots unfold in a setting that is, as contemporary reviewers noted, quintessentially gothic.

Although *Count Roderic's Castle* received notice in at least six contemporary reviews within a year of its publication in October of 1794, relatively little consensus emerges from the coverage. Ranging in length from a scant paragraph to nearly three pages, the reviews differ in approach and opinion. The longest of them, published by the *Literary Review*, is the least informative as a critical assessment; it comprises a plot summary (which unapologetically reveals all the major narrative surprises), and a lengthy excerpt, depicting the hero Rhinaldo in a characteristic scene of exploration through castle, tower, and tomb in the process of uncovering one of those surprises. The only qualitative judgment in the entire piece, the statement that the novel "ranks with the middle class of performances of the same description," is notable only for its studied neutrality (32). Other reviewers were less restrained. *The English Review,* for instance, the earliest periodical to offer an appraisal of the novel, dismissed the work in no uncertain terms. In its entirety, the review reads:

> This novel seems almost incomprehensible. It contains a continued scene of terrors, battles, and escapes; subterraneous vaults and men in irons; and ladies in distress. There have been so many such castles in the air that this is by no means new. It seems to be the intention of many of the novelists of the present day, as well as of former times, to outdo each other in the marvellous at any expence of probability. (392-3)

Such a review, negative as it sounds, is by no means anomalous for the gothic fiction of the 1790s. Reiterations of the common elements (terrors, battles, ladies in distress, and so forth) supposedly shared by these novels, and emphasis both on their numerousness and their morally or intellectually problematic aspects, are perhaps the most familiar refrains in 1790s fiction reviewing. *The Analytical Review* (1794) touches on some of the same themes, worrying that "The mind, as well as the body, loses it's [sic] sensibility ... by the too frequent reiteration of similar impressions" (488).

In other words, too much reading of genre fiction might not only blunt one's enjoyment of future literary efforts, but could inure a too-dedicated reader to the real-life sufferings of others. Comparing this kind of reading addiction to alcoholism, the reviewer bemoans the fact that this "class of readers" are "no longer capable of deriving pleasure from the gentle and tender sympathies of the heart" but "require to have their curiosity excited by artificial concealments, their astonishment kept awake by a perpetual succession of wonderful incidents, and their very blood congealed with chilling horrours" (489).[1] Yet the review closes on a positive note, albeit rather grudgingly: "The incidents," the writer concedes, "are numerous and well arranged; and the language is correct and elegant" (489). And the review ends there, for the reviewer claims that to include longer quotations, and explain them, would be to risk "forestalling the pleasure of perusing the whole by acquainting the reader before-hand with the plot," a concern which this introduction too shares (489).

Despite the mixed early reviews, the novel's popularity with readers who, reviewers' protests aside, clearly enjoyed the experience of having "their very blood congealed," is attested by the appearance of a second London edition before the end of the year,[2] and by 1795, even the tides of

1 Napier uses this characteristic review to open a discussion of the status of the gothic in the 1790s.
2 Garside et al., 1794:7 (Vol. 1, 103).

critical reception for the novel were shifting. North America embraced it, with editions published in both Philadelphia and Baltimore, and in April of that year both the *Monthly Review* and *The Critical Review* featured reviews, a fairly note-worthy occurrence given that gothic novels, and especially gothic novels published by the Minerva Press, were increas-ingly lucky to be noticed at all in the pages of these venerable reviews, let alone praised.[1]

The *Critical Review* compares *Count Roderic's Castle* to another Minerva novel reviewed on the same page, *The Duke of Clarence: An Historical Novel* (1795), declaring that *Count Roderic's Castle*, "like the preceding, treats of battles and murders, woods and fortresses, heroes and heroines. But the incidents are *somewhat* better connected, the style less inflated, and the superstitious terrors, which are introduced, as usual, to heighten the effect, are accounted for" without recourse to supernatural explanations (469). The *Monthly* reviewer goes even further. "In works of fiction," begins the review, "fertility of invention is unquestionably the first excellence; and this excellence the author of the romantic tale now before us certainly possesses" (466). Like earlier reviewers, this writer comments on the novel's "crowded succession of incidents," and refuses to give away key plot points, the revelation of which are said to "[rivet the read-er's] attention" and provide "new pleasure" (467). Perhaps the most interesting phrase in the entire review, however, opens its final sentence: "We shall therefore only remark that this tale is conceived with originality, and elegantly written", concluding that "those readers who can find pleasure in things new, strange, and terrible, will be much gratified by a visit to Count Roderic's Castle" (467). Can the same work be both "elegantly written" and "almost incomprehensible"? How can the same novel be at once "original" and one of

1 See, e.g., Roper 37 and Garside 16 on the increasing inability of reviews to pro-vide coverage for all novels in the late eighteenth century.

"many such castles in the air" or "too frequent reiteration[s] of similar impressions"? Even accepting the natural diversity of individual taste, and the likelihood that some reviewers may have been less than disinterested in their assessments, [1]the range of opinions represented here bears further consideration, pointing us to a central paradox in the reception of popular gothic fiction: what reviewers disparage in a novel may well be precisely what readers enjoy; moreover, the very familiarity of elements that strikes some readers as redundant and formulaic is a prerequisite for the comfortably reproducible—yet always newly surprising—reading experience that others prize.

The *English Review*'s assessment of *Count Roderic's Castle* as "incomprehensible" may be due in some degree to textual errors (for instance, the brief section in which Aspasia is suddenly, confusingly, and repeatedly, referred to as "Albina"). However, the substance of the complaint—"the continued scene of terrors, battles, and escapes; subterraneous vaults and men in irons"—is, like the *Analytical Review*'s claim that "[w]ithout allowing his reader time to breathe, the author conducts him from one gloomy castle, dismal dungeon, and dreary forest, to another" (489), at once a litany of recognizable gothic tropes and a kind of summary of the novel's narrative structure. Both the work's strength and its weakness, as its contemporary reviews suggest, the disorienting rapidity with which these familiar elements succeed each other is a dismaying sign of sensationalism for some and an innovative source of sensation for others.[2]

Count Roderic's Castle features a plot that advances by means of its characters apparently doing the same thing over and over again. The doubling that is so characteristic of gothic fiction here manifests dramatically in repeating

---

1 See Roper, chapter 1.
2 Napier's account of the "pace" of *Castle of Otranto* makes an interesting comparison here (88-92).

tropes and themes.[1] Indeed the repetition doesn't stop with doubling—in some cases, scenes repeat, albeit with significant variations, four or five times. Especially given the novel's relative brevity, its recursive quality creates a sense of *déjà vu* in the reader: haven't we been here before? haven't we seen this already? The characters' apparent unconsciousness of the recurring themes adds to their eeriness; while sometimes the protagonists don't have enough information to recognize things that the reader will (characters who haven't yet been to a particular dark forest mansion can't be expected to recognize it on sight), the easy acceptance, for instance, of the notable coincidence that no fewer than four of the characters have been held prisoner in the same out-of-the way ruin at various times in the novel, must strike the reader as peculiar. To experience the same thing over and over again, but not to recognize it (or at least not until it's too late) is the stuff of dreams or nightmares, and the plot does take on a fevered, nightmarish quality, as the characters flee from place to place, encountering the same terrors, and employing the same stratagems, over and over again.

One such stratagem is the use of disguise. Cases of mistaken or concealed identity are standard fare in 1790s gothic novels—whether a poor orphan unaware of his or her noble lineage or a demon masquerading as a young innocent, usually at least one person in any given novel is not what they seem. *Count Roderic's Castle* is no exception to this rule, but its characters exhibit an unusual affinity for sudden and deliberate disguise. Whereas the desire to conceal one's identity in

---

1 While varying from novel to novel, this characteristic Gothic pattern can manifest both in plot and in character. Botting argues that "Gothic excesses and transgressions repeatedly return to particular images and particular loci" (20), while Castle's description of Radcliffe's *Mysteries of Udolpho* focuses on characters, suggesting that they "mirror, or blur into one another ... Characters seem uncannily to resemble or to replace previous characters, sometimes in pairs" (126-127). The repetition in *Count Roderic's Castle* resembles this description more than, say, Botting's "monstrous double signifying duplicity and evil nature" (2); while there are certainly "evil" characters in the novel, heroes and heroines are just as—perhaps more—susceptible to narrative mirroring.

order to mislead or deceive others sometimes serves as a narrative hint about the morality of chameleon characters, such judgments here would disqualify most of the protagonists from hero or heroine status. The hero, Rhinaldo, murders a man by the second chapter, and the ambiguity of the act—it is portrayed as partially accidental, but Rhinaldo is only "astonished" rather than upset or regretful—is heightened by his immediate decision to assume his victim's identity:

> Rhinaldo, who now grew more anxious than ever to discover this mystery, took his resolution on the spot, and, with the assistance of Rugiero, stripping the doublet and cloak from the body of the man he had killed, he put them on, pulling his hair over his face, and disguising himself as artfully as he could with the blood which still flowed from the wound he had inflicted. He then put on Rugiero's hat, which…was well calculated to give extra concealment to his countenance. (14)

Especially given that the reader is hardly acquainted with Rhinaldo by this point in the text, the sudden murder, followed by the equally sudden decision to don the victim's clothes and smear himself with his blood, is unsettling, to say the least. His actions don't seem to strike anyone else as noteworthy, however, and his disguise serves its purpose. It is quickly revealed to be merely the first, if perhaps the most gruesome, of numerous similar scenes. His servant Rugiero is soon sent off on a mission of his own, during which he is instructed that "You had better … change dresses with this [woodman]. In his garb … you may easily gain admittance into the city" (36). Like his master, Rugiero takes to the suggestion with alacrity: "Rugiero immediately consented" and "disguised himself like a peasant" (36).

To disguise oneself may help to avoid detection, but it does not protect against deception by others. Rugiero's mission soon brings him to a room where he sees "a young man,

plainly drest, who seemed, as it appeared to Rugiero upon
entering, in the act of painting his face by a looking-glass
which stood on the table ... Such an employment, in such a
situation, could not fail to strike Rugiero" (39).

The reader too is naturally struck by this detail, which
foreshadows the eventual revelation of this new character's identity. As the plot continues to unfold, characters
disguise and reveal themselves in turn, creating a curious
tension between the novel's oft-repeated claim that truth
and honesty (or deception and villainy) are visible on the
countenance and the obvious expectation that disguises are
the most effective way of achieving one's aims. It is deemed
unremarkable that one character's "undisguised open
temper and demeanour" (114) should earn the trust of his
superiors, yet when Rhinaldo decides yet again "to disguise
himself" we are assured that his skills are such that "there
was little dread of his being discovered" (72). In a world
where every second person turns out to be in disguise, and
especially when those disguised are virtually all heroes or
heroines, never villains, how much credence can one place
on appearances?

The repeating habits of the characters are displayed
to advantage in a setting that features relatively few loca-
tions, which share uncanny similarities and are returned
to again and again. Take, for instance, that familiar gothic
novel trope, the mysterious ruin, hidden in the depths of
the woods. In the opening scene of the novel, Rhinaldo and
Rugiero come upon a seemingly abandoned structure, deep
in the forest. "[S]urely, my lord," said [Rugiero], "by the flash
of lightning, I just now descried the walls of a mansion"
(7). The gothic nature of the building soon reveals itself, as
"between some tall trees [Rhinaldo] thought he perceived
some rising turrets" (7); eerie and apparently abandoned,
it is variously described as "this mouldering bulwark" and
"of great antiquity" (8). The unexpected occurrences that

take place within the walls need no description here; most noteworthy is how closely tied the occurrences are to the spaces in which they unfold, and how the spaces themselves are encountered and reencountered. Some chapters later, a group of travelers have a similar experience: "they perceived a distant light glimmering through a vista in the forest ... they found themselves in a short time close to the walls of a spacious and stately castle" (45). And only a few pages after that, we find another similar scene: "they came to a more open part of the forest, a large and dark object before them, which they were soon convinced was, as indeed it proved ... an old and ruined mansion" (51). Over and over, groups of travelers (and the groups change and recombine through twists of plot, sometimes containing the same members, sometimes not) find themselves lost in the forest; over and over they catch sight of distant, mysterious, mansions and proceed towards them.

Two of these three sightings, it is eventually revealed, are of the same building, and while the "spacious and stately castle" is a different structure, it is nonetheless, we eventually learn, linked with the decrepit mansion through their ownership by two generations of the same family. The ruined mansion, then, is a kind of shadow version of the prosperous one—or a foreshadowing of its future.

As this final point suggests, what's especially fascinating about the repetitions that structure the novel is the way that the layerings work not just geographically (characters run and run but end up back exactly where they started), but *temporally*. Within the span of the plot, of course, characters take actions one after the other, but the author has constructed the narrative in such a way that repeated encounters with place also reveal a palimpsestic layering of events reaching back in time. Individual images, places, and scenes in the novel conform to this recursive structure, but it operates on a broader level as well: the novel concludes with Rhinaldo's righteous return to his father's residence—the very same "Count Roderic's Castle" from which he departed in the novel's first pages.

Without giving away too much of the plot, it is possible to consider one characteristically iterative figure: the chained noble prisoner (those "men in irons" identified by the *English Review*). The first action sequence in the novel, in the earliest-encountered forest mansion, culminates in the discovery of "as dismal a dungeon, as the most gloomy imagination could pourtray," from which Rhinaldo and Rugiero rescue "a man, seated on a large stone, to which he was chained" (19). That the prisoner turns out to be Rhinaldo's long-lost friend Count Tancred is typical of the plot's many coincidences; his liberation, however, is by no means the end of this dungeon, or mansion, for the plot. Rhinaldo himself is later held there, an experience that he recounts after his own rescue:

> [Rhinaldo's captor] ordered me to be conveyed to the dungeon from which I had rescued the Count Tancred … I heard the last door of my prison close—in vain did I wait to hear it open again—hour after hour passed away—and the horrid silence of the dungeon continued uninterrupted. My remorseless foes had doomed me to all the horrors of a death by famine (55).

As hero, Rhinaldo is of course not fated to starve, but the fact that he is held in the *same place* as his friend is crucial both to his survival (as he survives by drinking Tancred's forgotten water) and his eventual escape, effected by means of his own dagger, dropped during Tancred's rescue and abandoned. In the process of escaping, however, he encounters another, older, and less fortunate victim of the same plan:

> I discovered a rusty iron collar, chained to the wall—a hoop of iron, large enough to enclose the waist of a man, hung below it, close to the ground—and beneath it, amid a few

> rusted chains, and the tattered remnants of cloth which
> had escaped putrefaction, lay in a heap the skeleton of the
> wretch who had thus shrunk from his fetters. (56)

The clear implication that this discovery represents an alternate future for Rhinaldo himself is not left to the reader to deduce; it is only upon seeing the skeleton that Rhinaldo fully realizes his own intended fate, and declares "nor did I discover all the horrors of my former situation, 'till I found that the whole of the premises were deserted, and I was left to undergo the fate of the miserable victim, whose remains I had so lately beheld" (56).

As Volume One comes to a close, the narrator, in a seeming acknowledgement of the plot's recursive qualities thus far, declares that the characters have finally "left this forlorn mansion for ever!" (61), and this is true, so far as it goes. But while the characters don't return to the mansion again within the present time of the plot, we as readers keep revisiting it, and specifically revisiting the trope of men imprisoned there, through the flashbacks and narrated reminiscences of other characters. Tancred recounts his own imprisonment there again, reminding his listener as well as the reader that "I was the tenant of a loathsome dungeon, from which the hand of Providence, and the courage and conduct of my friend Rhinaldo, relieved me" (80-81). Still another character, who shall here remain nameless, eventually reveals his own previous captivity within the same mansion. While this character's experience differs in some aspects, the description of his captivity and eventual escape through a mysterious crack in the wall echoes Rhinaldo's own experience, which takes place earlier in the novel, but later in time.

Thus the characters circle back again and again to the same places, while also cycling through the same experiences. As the reader eventually realizes, the places that seem fraught with such meaning are often so because *the same thing has already happened there*. The dreamlike quality of the setting (and perhaps the plausibility of the characters' unwitting reenactments) is heightened by the profusion of vague details about the gothic interiors through which the characters move. In the first scenes in the abandoned mansion, just as in the scenes in Book Two that take place in Count Roderic's castle, the movements of the characters through rooms, up and down staircases, through trapdoors, and along corridors is described in a way that is at once extremely precise and utterly bewildering. The spatial orientations and layouts of the buildings are nearly impossible to envision, despite (or possibly because of) the excessive details of the characters' movements up, down, passing, bumping into, above and below each other.[1] If the reader persists in following the characters as they move about, the result is a kind of disorientation, an indistinguishable tangle of dark rooms, shadowy figures, and distant lights that one is unequipped to navigate. As the secrets of the buildings slowly reveal themselves to Rhinaldo and the others, the spatial confusion slowly resolves as well, until persons and objects once obscure finally resolve themselves into clear and fixed entities. We might thus see readerly confusion as a deliberate strategy, one that, to some degree, forces the reader into the same state of uncertainty that the characters inhabit.[2]

Even as *Count Roderic's Castle* deals in gothic clichés, then—disguised characters and ruined mansions, convents, murders, strange repetitions and dreamlike scenes of terror and confusion—it retains an unsettling edge, an energy that

1 See Howells 26: "[Gothic] [s]cenery shifts arbitrarily from one episode to the next; this is not merely related to the conventions of romance landscape but more fundamentally to the general instability and impermanence of things ... melting back into the landscape of nightmare." See also Napier on the "precise delineation of physical space" in *Castle of Otranto*: "The amount of movement here is so obviously exaggerated that it impedes a reflective response on the part of the reader" (38).

2 Haggerty suggests that "the most obvious yet profound fact about Gothic fiction" is that "its primary formal aim is the emotional and psychological involvement of the reader" (18).

derives from its dense compression of certain tropes and its eschewal of others.[1] No giant helmets or ghosts with booming voices crash into the prose, à la *The Castle of Otranto*; the novel's convent scenes are notably devoid of either inquisitions or cruel Mother Superiors. Nature is there to be gotten through on one's way to somewhere else, not to inspire flights of fancy or rhapsodic descriptions, and supernatural apparitions tend to be demystified in a matter of paragraphs rather than at volume's end. The fears and joys of characters are conveyed as briefly as possible, and while Rhinaldo is clearly the hero of the tale, we are by no means led to identify with him or enter into his thoughts as we are with a heroine like Radcliffe's Emily St. Aubert. Indeed, characterization itself is not something on which the author spends much time: the characters are all relatively flat, and the narrator, while theoretically omniscient, offers little access to their motivations or to any thoughts that don't relate to straightforward actions or reactions: fear, joy, desire to carry out a plan.[2]

All of the characters in a given category (male protagonist; villain; female love interest) are fairly indistinguishable in terms of personality, and the women in particular are notably underdeveloped. With the exception of a few minor scenes, they are pawns and prizes in the novel's masculine political games, on the scene to be kidnapped, rescued, or swoon in terror, but never to advance the action on their own. The force and energy of this novel lies in the action, and, as the castle of the title suggests, the action is closely tied to the buildings—sometimes ruined, sometimes royal, sometimes horrifying, sometimes liberating—in which it

---

1 Cf. Haggerty: "The devices typical of gothic fiction have not been chosen by accident ... they have the power to objectify subjective states of feeling. [...] gothic form, then, is affective form" (8).

2 Such characterization is extremely common in Gothic novels; Howells, for instance, notes that Gothic authors "tend to concentrate on external details of emotional display while leaving readers to deduce for themselves complex inner psychological movements" (15).

unfolds. A characteristic work of early genre fiction, *Count Roderic's Castle* is that counterintuitive creature: a novel that already felt thoroughly familiar upon its publication in 1794, yet whose "succession of surprising and terrible adventures" (in the words of the *Analytical Review*) still has the power to surprise readers today.

HANNAH DOHERTY HUDSON

WORKS CITED

Birkhead, Edith. *Tale of Terror: A Study of the Gothic Romance*. New York: Russell & Russell, 1963.

Blakey, Dorothy. *The Minerva Press*. London: The Bibliographical Society at the Oxford University Press, 1939.

Botting, Fred. *Gothic*. London and New York: Routledge, 1996.

Castle, Terry, *The Female Thermometer: Eighteenth Century Culture and the Invention of the Uncanny*. New York and Oxford: Oxford University Press, 1995.

Clery, E.J. "The Genesis of Gothic Fiction." *The Cambridge Companion to Gothic Fiction*. Edited by Jerrold Hogle. Cambridge and New York: Cambridge University Press 2002. 21-39.

—. *The Rise of Supernatural Fiction, 1762-1800*. Cambridge: Cambridge University Press, 1995.

Ellis, Kate Ferguson. *The Contested Castle: Gothic Novels and the Subversion of Domestic Ideology*. Champaign, Ill.: University of Illinois Press, 1989.

Haggerty, George E. *Gothic Fiction/Gothic Form*. University Park: Pennsylvania State University Press, 1989.

Gamer, Michael. *Romanticism and the Gothic: Genre, Reception, and Canon Formation*. Cambridge: Cambridge University Press, 2000.

Garside, Peter. "The English Novel in the Romantic Era: Consolidation and Dispersal." *The English Novel, 1770-1829: A Bibliographical Survey of Prose Fiction Published in the British Isles*. Edited by Peter Garside, James Raven, and Rainer

Schöwerling. Vol. 2. Oxford and New York: Oxford University Press, 2000.

Garside, Peter, James Raven, and Rainer Schöwerling, eds. *The English Novel, 1770-1829: A Bibliographical Survey of Prose Fiction Published in the British Isles*. 2 vols. Oxford: Oxford University Press, 2000

Howells, Coral Ann. *Love, Mystery, and Misery: Feeling in Gothic Fiction*. London: Athlone Press, 1978.

Jockers, Matthew Lee. *Macroanalysis: Digital Methods and Literary History*. Urbana: University of Illinois Press, 2013.

Lynch, Deidre S. "Gothic Fiction." *The Cambridge Companion to Fiction in the Romantic Period*, edited by Richard Maxwell and Katie Trumpener, 47-63. Cambridge: Cambridge University Press, 2008.

McLeod, Deborah. "The Minerva Press." Unpublished Ph.D. dissertation, University of Alberta, 1997.

Miles, Robert. *Ann Radcliffe: The Great Enchantress*. Manchester: Manchester University Press. New York, 1995.

—. *Gothic Writing, 1750-1820: A Genealogy*. London: Routledge, 1993.

—. "The 1790s: the Effulgence of Gothic." *The Cambridge Companion to Gothic Fiction*. Edited by Jerrold Hogle. Cambridge and New York: Cambridge University Press 2002. 41-62.

Moretti, Franco. "Style, Inc. Reflections on Seven Thousand Titles (British Novels, 1740-1850)." *Critical Inquiry* 36.1 (2009): 134-158.

Napier, Elizabeth. *The Failure of Gothic: Problems of Disjunction in an Eighteenth-Century Literary Form*. Oxford: Clarendon Press, 1987.

Norton, Rictor. *Mistress of Udolpho: The Life of Ann Radcliffe*. London: Leicester University Press, 1999.

Punter, David. *The Literature of Terror: A History of Gothic Fictions from 1765 to the Present Day*. New York: Longman, 1980.

Raven, James. "Historical Introduction: The Novel Comes of Age." *The English Novel, 1770-1829: A Bibliographical Survey of Prose Fiction Published in the British Isles*. Edited by Peter Garside, James Raven, and Rainer Schöwerling. Vol. 1. Oxford and New York: Oxford University Press, 2000.

Review of *Count Roderic's Castle, or, Gothic Times, a Tale*. *The Literary Review and Historical Journal* 2 (10 January 1795): 32-34.

Review of *Count Roderic's Castle, or, Gothic Times, a Tale*. *The British Critic* 5 (June 1795): 665-666.

Review of *Count Roderic's Castle, or, Gothic Times, a Tale*. *The Analytical Review* 20.4 (Dec. 1794): 488-489.

Review of *Count Roderic's Castle, or, Gothic Times, a Tale*. *The English Review* 24 (Nov. 1794): 392-393.

Review of *Count Roderic's Castle, or, Gothic Times, a Tale*. *The Monthly Review* 16 (April 1795): 466-467.

Review of *Count Roderic's Castle, or, Gothic Times, a Tale*. *The Critical Review* 13 (April 1795): 469.

Roper, Derek. *Reviewing Before the Edinburgh, 1788-1802*. London: Methuen, 1978.

Summers, Montague. *The Gothic Quest: A History of the Gothic Novel*. New York: Russell & Russell, 1964.

Sedgwick, Eve Kosofsky. *The Coherence of Gothic Conventions*. New York: Methuen, 1986.

St. Clair, William. *The Reading Nation in the Romantic Period*. Cambridge and New York: Cambridge University Press, 2004.

Tompkins, J.M.S. *The Popular Novel in England, 1770-1800*. London: Methuen and Co., 1961.

Watt, James. *Contesting the Gothic: Fiction, Genre, and Cultural Conflict, 1764-1832*. Cambridge: Cambridge University Press, 1999.

NOTE ON THE TEXT

This edition follows the text of the original two-volume edition published by William Lane's Minerva Press in London in 1794. No effort has been made to modernize spelling or punctuation; however, a small number of obvious printer's errors have been silently corrected. The author occasionally loses track of his characters, too, referring once to Ellenor as "Isabel" and calling Rhodolpho "Astolpho" once by mistake; these have been corrected for clarity's sake; however, the error referred to in the introduction ("Aspasia" / "Albina") has been retained as in the original text.

COUNT RODERIC's
CASTLE:

OR,

GOTHIC TIMES,

A TALE.

IN TWO VOLUMES.

VOL. I.

In winter's tedious nights, fit by the fire,
With good old folks, and let them tell thee tales
Of woeful ages long ago betide.

SHAK. RICH. II.

LONDON:

PRINTED FOR WILLIAM LANE,

AT THE

Minerva=Press,

LEADENHALL-STREET.

MDCCXCIV.

Frontispiece to an undated mid-19th century American reprint, retitled
Rinaldo and Isabel; or, Count Roderic's Castle: An Italian Romance
(Philadelphia: J.B. Perry). Collection of the Publisher.

COUNT RODERIC's CASTLE.

CHAP. I.

IN those days when Astolpho, surnamed the Proud, beheld his regal sway extend over the rich and fertile plains of Lombardy, the name of Roderic the Hardy was not unknown to fame. He had fought the battles of the empire; and an almost uninterrupted series of success had crowned his arms. He had acquired immortal honour to himself, and a vast accession of territory to his master; but wholly trained in the field of war, and little skilled in the cabals of a court, he found, after a life almost exhausted in the painful pursuits of glory, the smiles of the king's countenance withdrawn.

He no sooner witnessed the dangerous gloom which began to thicken around him, than he prepared to pursue those steps which were most likely to conduce to his safety, and lead him to an asylum in which he might, in all probability, find a shelter from the gathering storm. He retired, then, while it was yet safe to retire, from the capital, and sought a castle of his own near the frontiers of a lately conquered province—a retreat, in which the bolts of Astolpho's wrath were but little likely to reach him. To this retirement he summoned an only son, whom he had left behind him in the army, and who, though but a young soldier, had already acquired a portion of fame little inferior to that of his father.

This son, who was called Rhinaldo, had been, during the intervals which occurred between each campaign, much resident at court, and in the palace of Astolpho first beheld the lady Isabel, the daughter of the late king, and loved her. It would have been difficult indeed for a young man of the coldest heart to behold her without emotion. In her dark eyes were mingled all the fire of genius with all the softness of sensibility; on her animated countenance sate blended majesty and mildness; on her brow was pictured command-ing beauty; in her smile the most winning sweetness; her shape was faultless, and her demeanour artless and graceful; nor was Isabel blind to the merits of the young soldier—a person the very standard of manly beauty—a countenance, where every virtue of his heart was pourtrayed——a cul-tivated mind—a high and unspotted reputation, did not escape the observation of the lady Isabel. They had frequent opportunities of conversing, and of those opportunities a mutual passion was the result.

The resentment of Astolpho became implacable, when he heard of Count Roderic's retreat; and the very day after Rhinaldo had, in obedience to his father's mandates, quitted the army to join him in his retirement, orders arrived at the camp to supersede him in his command, and cause him to be conveyed close prisoner to the capital.

These orders had, indeed, been preceded by a letter from the lady Isabel, warning Rhinaldo of the danger which threatened him;—a letter, rendered not more dear to Rhi-naldo by the noble proof it contained, than by the tender vows it breathed, of inviolable fidelity.

In the retirement which his father had chosen, Rhinaldo passed many melancholy hours in meditating on his beloved but absent Isabel. In vain did Count Roderic endeavour to divert his thoughts from the ceaseless object of their atten-tion, by dissertations on that science in which this beloved son had, from the earliest period of life, been his pupil, and in which they had both gained so great a degree of renown. In vain did he encourage, among his men at arms, (for he carried into retirement with him a retinue, which caused no little jealousy at court,) those martial exercises for their courage and dexterity in which the men of that age were renowned. In vain did the court of the Castle echo daily with the sound of the trumpet.—In vain were the banners seen waving above the battlements. That heart which had so often leaped at the sound of martial music, which owned no charms but those which blazed in the front of an embattled host, now shrunk from what it deemed a tedious mockery, and sought to indulge its feelings amid the luxury of the most gloomy solitude.

A deep and devious forest, which flanked the Castle to the south, afforded this solitude, and thither did Rhinaldo daily repair to feast his imagination on the thousand charms with which the image of his Isabel was replete. His father, who discovered his dislike of society, and probably in some measure guessed at the cause of it, forbore, at length, to restrain his inclination. They seldom met but at table, (from the tasteless festivity of which Rhinaldo retired as soon as decency would permit him,) or at those hours when the public duties of religion summoned them to the neighbouring convent.

At these duties Rhinaldo was so constant, and his attention to them was so rigid and undeviating, that his father could not forbear entertaining some fears, that his melancholy would at length enroll him among the religious of the place. Nor were those fears entertained upon light or frivolous grounds. The society consisted of thirty persons, who had all borne arms with a considerable degree of reputation. The superior was an old knight, who had led Roderic himself in the field, and had been his guide in the path of glory, though he was yet, from a youth, inured to toil, and an age fostered by temperance, vigorous and hardy. But the person, the charms of whose society so frequently led the steps of Rhinaldo towards the Convent, was an hermit, who had built his cell hard by, and whose disposition, truly charitable, had rendered him highly respected, as well by the monks themselves, as by the scattered inhabitants of the neighbourhood.

The convent of St. Julian was situate close to Count Roderic's Castle, on a bold and commanding eminence.—Consisting chiefly of rock, it seemed scarcely capable of affording nourishment to the numerous shrubs, whose twisted roots seemed incorporated with it, and was accessible only by a winding path of considerable length. Steep, rugged, and intricate, it was a task of considerable labour to gain the summit, whose picturesque appearance, from the vale below, never failed to incite in the mind an ardent wish to attain it.

The flinty walls of the Convent seemed to have their foundation in air, and its gothic spires hung over the brow of the rock with an awful magnificence. It overlooked the Castle. This, as the latter was a place of strength, was a circumstance of importance, and extreme care was taken, on any prospect of an attack, to secure this post, and to afford it ample supplies.

Beneath a projecting part of the cliff, close to the winding path already mentioned, and at no great distance from the summit, had the hermit, of whose society young Rhinaldo was so fond, fixed his abode. His daily care, during the period of his residence in that spot, when the duties of religion had been fulfilled, was to enlarge, amend, and decorate his humble cell, till he had at length formed an habitation, which, for simple beauty and comfort, the thoughtless inhabitant of the gay world might envy him.

To this retreat, then, did Rhinaldo fly from the cumberous magnificence of Count Roderic's establishment.—Here could he meditate at leisure on the virtues and accomplishments of his beloved Isabel. Here too (and it was that circumstance which rendered the spot so dear to him) could he confide, without the dread of cold sarcasm, or harsh reproof, the tender secret of his heart. Father Anthony (for that was the hermit's name) was austere indeed towards himself, but, like the holy master, to whose service he had now devoted himself, he wept over the failings of others.

CHAP. II.

S OME months had now passed since Rhinaldo quitted his command to retire to the Castle of his father, and his visits to the hermitage had grown daily more and more frequent, when one morning at the approach of dawn, he ordered the draw-bridge to be let down, and, attended only by one faithful servant, took the road which led to the capital. They passed the day in tracing the thick and impervious forest which cloaths for many miles the southern frontier of that kingdom, and the shades of evening overtook them as they gained its verge. The night set in with unwonted darkness, and the chill gust, which began to howl from the north, foretold an approaching tempest. A few drops of thick rain fell—the darkness redoubled—the distant thunder began to growl——Rhinaldo gave his horse the reins, and trusting to the sagacity of this long-tried favourite for his safety, he proceeded at a slow pace, attended by his faithful servant, catching every now and then a glimpse of the wild scene around, by the gleam of the lightning, which began to dart with almost unabating rapidity.

Rugiero (so was Rhinaldo's servant called) stopped his horse suddenly, and called to his master; "surely, my lord," said he, "by the flash of lightning, I just now descried the walls of a mansion."

Rhinaldo stopped. Rugiero bade him look to the right, and between some tall trees he thought he perceived some rising turrets. They turned their horses, and made slowly and cautiously for the spot. As they drew near, they found that their surmises were true.—They pursued their route, and at length, with considerable difficulty, arrived at the gate of an old mansion.

Like most of the seats of the nobility in that kingdom, it was surrounded by a moat. Rugiero alighted from his horse, and slowly began to trace the moat round, to discover, if possible, a bridge over which they might pass, and at least gain some shelter from the inclemency of the night. He had not proceeded far, before he perceived, on the opposite side, a draw-bridge drawn up, which made him conjecture, that, desolate as the building appeared, (for the walls were in several parts overgrown with thick ivy, and bore every mark, as far as the light would permit them to be discovered, of great antiquity) it was inhabited.

He began now to halloo as loud as he could, but with little probability, from the howling of the storm, of making himself heard. He continued his progress along the margin of the moat, and Rhinaldo, having alighted from his horse, slowly followed him.—They had not proceeded far, before they discovered that this outwork bore as strong marks of decay as the rest of the building, and that the raising the draw-bridge at night must be more a work of custom than utility.

Rugiero, by a very easy, but broken descent, gained the moat, and boldly stepped into it. He found it very shallow, and ascending upon the ruins which had fallen from a low and crumbling wall on the other side, he gained the opposite bank. He then returned to give his master notice of this circumstance, and to conduct him over. Rhinaldo did not hesitate; taking his horse in his hand, he followed his servant. The beasts sprung lightly from the ruins upon the crazy remains of this mouldering bulwark, and the travellers, passing slowly round the walls of the house, arrived at a large and lofty porch, over-hung with ivy, and mid-leg deep in the grass, which grew thro' the crevices of the stones with which it had been paved. Having fastened their horses to a thorn which grew close to one of the pillars, they retired to the extremity of the porch for shelter. This shelter, however, they did not find—the rain beat in upon them with violence.

Rhinaldo resolved to try if the door was open. It was not improbable that it should be so, even if the mansion were inhabited. In a place so desolate, there is little fear of interlopers, and the moat and draw-bridge would probably render the domestics careless.—He raised a weighty latch, and putting his shoulder against the door, it opened heavily; and Rhinaldo and his servant entered. Rhinaldo still held the door in his hand, and firmly persuaded, from every thing he had hitherto witnessed, that the house was uninhabited, ordered Rugiero to conduct the horses into the hall, where he determined to rest for the night.

Rugiero strenuously advised him to learn first, whether the mansion were actually inhabited or no; and with this advice, upon consideration, he thought it best to comply. He hallooed aloud, but the storm seemed to mock his efforts. He walked slowly across the hall, but stopping suddenly, exclaimed, "Rugiero, are these your footsteps which I hear?" "No, my Lord," answered Rugiero, "I have not moved from this spot." "There is somebody," continued Rhinaldo, "ascending a flight of stairs."

He now hallooed again; when a hoarse voice, in a low tone, exclaimed, "peace, fool! are you fit to be trusted with a secret of such importance?" Still all was dark; the sound of the footsteps on the staircase died gradually away, and left Rhinaldo much perplexed. "Stay here," said he, after a pause, to Rugiero, "till I return."

Rugiero remonstrated, but his master was peremptory, and this attendant had studied discipline in a camp. "I will be cautious," said Rhinaldo, mildly, in order to soften the apprehension of his faithful servant. "At all events, your remaining here will secure us a retreat, should any thing sinister occur."

Rhinaldo now advanced, and tracing his way slowly and

cautiously along the hall, reached at length the staircase, from which the words, which so much awakened his curiosity, had proceeded. He judged that this staircase, though now somewhat crazy from age, had once been magnificent. It was very spacious. He had scarcely got half way up it, when he heard footsteps above him, as if of some person descending. He stood motionless, in hopes that, whoever it might be, from the size of the staircase they would pass without detecting him; for the mystery of persons thus moving in the dark perplexed him even more than the singular speech he had heard, and he was more than ever anxious to discover the cause of it. The footsteps now seemed advancing towards him; he moved a pace to the right, in order to avoid a meeting, and placed himself just in the way of the person descending, who jostled him. A voice immediately exclaimed, "Gaspard, why do you not speak? You must either bawl or be dumb—the house is locked in sleep—you may now strike a light—meet me, ten minutes hence, in the refectory."

Rhinaldo was now divided what to do—when a light, the only one he had yet discovered, gleaming dimly from the door of a chamber into a long gallery above, determined him to pursue his way up the staircase. He proceeded lightly and cautiously. The light in a short time disappeared, but he bent his steps towards the place whence it had proceeded. He could discover this place to be a spacious chamber, for through a door which opened into a passage at the farther end of it, he again saw a faint ray of light. He crossed the chamber, and entered the passage, at the farther end of which he just distinguished the legs of a man ascending a narrow staircase. He followed with extreme caution, and saw this person enter a small room at the top of the staircase, which seemed to be a repository for very old battered and unserviceable armour, and worn-out horse-furniture. The person he had followed passed strait to the end of the room, and Rhinaldo gained such a height on the staircase, as to see him shove back a pannel of the wainscot, which seemed artificially contrived for the purpose of concealment, and pulling a bunch of keys from his pocket, open a strong massy door, plated with iron; he then descended a few steps, shutting it after him, and Rhinaldo lost sight of him.

Perplexed at this circumstance, he advanced some paces towards the iron door. He listened, and thought he could hear the sound of voices; but it was so indistinct, that he was left at last in doubt whether he had not been deceived; and recollecting the conversation which passed on the staircase, he resolved to return and rejoin Rugiero, with whom perhaps he might discover what was to be perpetrated in the refectory. He groped his way down again, and at his post he found his servant, who, the moment he came near him, grasped his hand, and bade him, in a low whisper, be silent and watch.

They had not stood many minutes before they perceived a faint light gleam from an arch way on the opposite side of the hall, and two figures advancing slowly along a passage, one of whom carried a kind of dark lanthorn. They perceived them to be men meanly dressed, and of the most unprepossessing appearance; one particularly, whose profusion of coarse, long, black hair, was unpleasingly contrasted with the livid paleness of his countenance, excited Rhinaldo's attention.

In a hoarse and dissonant voice, but which Rhinaldo discovered to be the same which had addressed him on the staircase, he exclaimed, "Hark! I heard something." "'Twas nothing but the wind," replied the other.—"Hist!" exclaimed the first, and paused; "where are the servants?" "Locked in sleep," said the other.—They now placed their light on a table just within the arch way, and the man who had spoke first, said to the other, "why did not you answer me, when I met you on the staircase?" "When?" said the other. "Just now—within these ten minutes." "I never met you—I have not been up stairs."——"Lyar!" exclaimed the first. "May I fall dead this instant," returned the second, "if I have left the refectory. Hey! what ails you? you tremble." "No matter," exclaimed the first, in a faltering voice. "Give me the bottle." He took a small wicker bottle from the other, and drank from it. It seemed to revive him. "Give me the lanthorn," said he, "and the dagger." He received from him the dark lanthorn, and a dagger of some length, which he stuck in his girdle. "Shall you want me?" asked the second man. "No," said the first; "go—wait for my lord—we shall not want you, 'till the body is to be disposed of."——"Mercy on us!" cried the second, in an awful but tremulous tone. The first turned short round upon him, muttered something between his teeth, and walked slowly across the hall towards another passage, while the second man moved towards the staircase, which he ascended.

Rhinaldo and Rugiero, with as little noise as possible, followed the first man; yet they could not proceed so silently, but that they caused him to turn round several times. The loudness of the storm, however, deceived him, and he continued to move forward, through a winding passage, 'till he stopped suddenly at a low arched door, which he opened with a key.

Rhinaldo drew his sword, and rushed forward to prevent his shutting it again. This, however, he did not attempt, and Rhinaldo gained the door, just as he had placed the lanthorn on the floor, in the middle of a small vaulted room, and seemed occupied in thought. He stood with his arms folded, and his face turned towards Rhinaldo. Never was a countenance so ghastly and horrid. It betrayed a most diabolical agitation of mind. After standing thus for a few seconds, he stooped down, and, feeling along the floor, laid hold of an iron ring, by which, after a few efforts, he pulled up a trap door, and discovered, by the gleam of the lanthorn, a broken flight of steps. He now took up the lanthorn in one hand, and holding the door with the other, began to descend. Rhinaldo saw that there was not a moment to be lost. If this ruffian should once get beneath the trap-door, the murder he meant to perpetrate (and of his intention there could not remain a doubt) might be committed in safety. Impressed with this idea, he sprung forward. The man turned around at the noise, and on the instant received Rhinaldo's sword to the very hilt in his breast. He fell into the vault, uttering a deep groan—the lanthorn was clenched in his hand—the trap-door fell into its place as he descended, and Rhinaldo, with Rugiero, who had just entered the room, remained involved in the most impenetrable darkness.

CHAP. III.

A STONISHED at this circumstance, Rhinaldo paused for a few seconds; but recollecting that it was possible the light might not be extinguished by the fall, he felt for the iron ring, and lifted the trap-door. His conjectures proved to be right—the lanthorn lay on the floor, clasped in the hand of the dead man—and the flame within it was burning the horn. Rugiero picked it up, and having adjusted the candle within it, began to survey the vault into which they had descended.

It was narrow, long, and low; and at the end of it was a very small arched door-way, and a door apparently very thick, and formidably secured with bolts and bars. Rugiero pushed the door with his hand, and was suddenly alarmed by a deep groan from the place, whatever it might be, to which it opened. He had not time, however, to ruminate long on this circumstance; his master called to him in a very low voice from the other end of the vault, and when he came near, made him a sign to listen; he did so, and heard distinctly the footsteps of a man walking in a hasty and agitated step over their heads. Every now and then he paused, as if to listen to something; and after a few minutes, they heard exclaiming in a low tone "Fabian!"

This was repeated several times;—and Rhinaldo at length perceiving that it was addressed towards the vault, answered in as hollow a voice as he could assume, "Here!"

"Is it done?" exclaimed the unknown person from above. "It is," answered Rhinaldo. "'Tis well," resumed the voice from above. "Convey the body into the vaulted room—lay it out on the table, and cover it with the mantle which I shall send you."—They then heard the steps of this person moving towards the door, and the sound of them soon died away.

Rhinaldo, who now grew more anxious than ever to discover this mystery, took his resolution on the spot, and, with the assistance of Rugiero, stripping the doublet and cloak from the body of the man he had killed, he put them on, pulling his hair over his face, and disguising himself as artfully as he could with the blood which still flowed from the wound he had inflicted. He then put on Rugiero's hat, which being much plainer than his own, was well calculated to give additional concealment to his countenance; and, with the assistance of this steady and faithful domestic, lifting the trap-door, conveyed the body into the vaulted chamber above, and stretched it on the table as directed.

This done, they prepared to secure the messenger who should be sent with the mantle, and who they judged would prove the person they had before seen in company with the man who was slain. In order to effect this, Rugiero, drawing his sword, placed himself close to the door of the room, just within the portal, while his master stood at the front of the table, on which the body was placed, and so much in front of the lanthorn, which he had contrived should throw but a dim gleam of light, that a person entering the room, could only distinguish the figure of a man, but was not enabled to discover who, or what he might be.

They had not waited on their post many minutes before, as they had conjectured, the person they so lately saw entered the room, carrying the mantle on his shoulders. He walked strait towards Rhinaldo, to whom he said,—"Fabian! my Lord requires you to attend him at the head of the great staircase."

He had scarcely uttered these words, before Rugiero, advancing from the door, seized him by the collar, and Rhinaldo doing the same, the fellow fell down speechless with horror. They raised him immediately, and Rhinaldo warned him, that to utter a single exclamation would prove fatal to him.—He fell on his knees, and in the most earnest manner entreated them to spare his life. Rhinaldo told him that his safety wholly depended on his conduct. "Disguise nothing from us," said he, "and you have nothing to fear."—"Sir," said the trembling wretch, "I will conceal nothing, but my Lord, by this time, waits for Fabian and myself, at the head of the great staircase." After a moment's pause, Rhinaldo said, "I think I can trust thee so far. Thou shalt attend me to thy Lord—but mark well my words—the very moment in which, by a single word or action, thou attemptest to betray me, I here swear, whatever may be the consequence of it, shall be the last of thy life."

Rhinaldo then threw the mantle over the body of the ghastly Fabian, and commanding the trembling wretch before him to conduct him to the great staircase, he gave the lanthorn into his hands, ordering him to precede him a few paces, but, at his peril, to keep the light turned from him.

In this manner they proceeded, leaving Rugiero in the vaulted room.—They had scarcely gained the foot of the staircase, before they perceived a man walking at the top of it, with a small taper in his hand. He was richly drest, but had a ferocity in his aspect that did not escape unmarked by

Rhinaldo, who kept as much behind his conductor as possible.

The man at the head of the staircase no sooner perceived them, than he ordered them, in an impatient tone, to follow him, and turning hastily, walked along the gallery, into which the gleam of light had led the steps of Rhinaldo, when he was last on the staircase. He passed through the same chamber which he had before passed, entered the passage, ascended the narrow staircase, and shoved back the pannel in the little room above it. He then opened the door, and discovered to Rhinaldo a scene, which excited his utmost attention. A few steps descended from the door he had opened into a lofty and spacious apartment, the furniture of which, though one could perceive that it had been once magnificent, appeared very old and decayed.

At a table on which was placed a dim lamp and a crucifix, he could perceive a lady richly drest. Her elbow rested on the table, and her cheek on her hand. She was reading. The man who preceded Rhinaldo turned to him and his companion, and ordered them to stay without. He then proceeded down the steps. The lady cast her eyes towards him as he entered, threw them with a supplicating look towards heaven, and again fixed them on her book.

He advanced slowly into the room, and beckoning the lady, in a stern tone of voice ordered her to follow him.

"What more am I to suffer?" said she. "What farther scene of savage cruelty am I to witness?"

He beckoned Rhinaldo and his companion into the room. The lady started wildly when she saw them. "Nay," said she, "if I am to be murdered, perpetrate your crime on this spot."—Saying this, she seized the crucifix; clasped it to her bosom, and fell on her knees before the book, which lay open on the table. The person who had caused this alarm then took her under one arm, and making a sign to Rhinaldo to do the same by the other, she suffered herself to be conducted, without a murmur, whithersoever they should choose, still holding the crucifix in her hand.

Rhinaldo, struck with compassion at the situation of this lady, was repeatedly tempted to whisper comfort in her ear; but he thought a premature discovery of his design might in all probability baffle every attempt he might make to serve her; he therefore proceeded, holding her still by the arm, 'till they gained the vaulted chamber, when the person who had conducted her to it thus addressed her: "Adulteress!"—She raised herself from the arm of Rhinaldo. "Monster!" said she, "at least, spare my fame—thou knowest the falshood of that insinuation."——"That mantle,"—said he, pointing to that which lay over the body of Fabian, "was the work of your hands, and designed doubtless as a present to me." "Never,"—answered the lady,—"heaven knows.—They to whose power it was my lot to bow, knew too well that it was not designed for thee."

"Perhaps," returned he, with an air of the most savage triumph, "it was designed for him who now wears it." At this the lady started——she looked wild with apprehension and terror—she advanced towards the table—she clasped her hands together, and eagerly looked on the mantle—"It cannot be," said she—"you are not such a monster." The man advanced, and with a barbarous readiness, seized the taper which his attendant carried, and held it before her. "Lift up the mantle," said he, to Rhinaldo. Rhinaldo lifted it, fixing his eyes full upon him, and discovered the body of Fabian.

"Good heavens!" cried the lady; "what can all this mean?" She staggered some paces back, and was caught in the arms of Rugiero, who had advanced to be ready to assist his master upon occasion.——The man himself seemed petrified with astonishment upon seeing the corpse—in a few seconds he drew his sword.

"Consummate villain!" said he; and he flew at Rhinaldo. Rhinaldo, who watched his eye, drew at the same time, beat down the thrust which was made, with extreme rapidity, at his breast, and, returning it, buried his sword in his adversary's body; but perceived, on recovering his guard, that he was himself wounded in the thigh; he, however, advanced towards the lady, and seeing her somewhat recovered, attempted to explain to her that the person for whose life she seemed to labour under such apprehensions, was probably safe—but he poured this intelligence into a deaf ear. Harrassed to death by the cruelties of her oppressor, and the scene she had witnessed, she seemed insensible to all around her.—Rhinaldo and Rugiero conducted her slowly to the apartment in which they had found her, and placed her on the bed.

Rhinaldo then inquired whether there were any female servants in the house, and hearing that there were two, he went, attended by the companion of the deceased Fabian, to awaken them, and in a short time procured their attendance on the lady.

After taking care that every possible assistance should be given to her, Rhinaldo turned his thoughts once more towards the vaulted chamber, and leaving the lady under the protection of his faithful Rugiero, he ordered Gaspard (for so was Fabian's comrade called) to attend him; and again proceeded down the stairs, determined to explore the vault, in which the miscreant, he had so lately punished, had met the reward of his iniquities.

As they entered the room, the first object that struck them was the body of the person who had just fallen by Rhinaldo's sword. Rhinaldo held the taper to his face, and contemplating his features, though now fixed by the agonies of death,— "Is not this," said he, to Gaspard, "the Lord of St. Amand?" Gaspard answered in the affirmative. Rhinaldo felt the body; but no signs of life remained. He then ordered Gaspard to raise the trap-door, and followed him into the vault. They proceeded along this dreary subterraneous passage, 'till they came to the little door at the end. This, after some labour, they unbolted, for the fastenings were numerous and strong, and descending by a narrow broken staircase, entered as dismal a dungeon, as the most gloomy imagination could pourtray.

In one corner they descried the figure of a man, seated on a large stone, to which he was chained. As they opened the door, he cast a languid eye towards them, and exclaimed, "I shall at last then find an end to my miseries! Do not fear to perform your commission—but, if you have any compassion left, bear the ring which you will find in my bosom to the wife of your lord."

Rhinaldo advanced towards him.—"Have you," resumed the prisoner, "compassion enough to promise me that favour?" "Count Tancred!" said Rhinaldo, astonished at the voice which addressed him. "My friend—my——"

The prisoner leaped in surprise from his seat, but, restrained by his chains, he sunk down again. "Know ye not Rhinaldo?" said the young knight, and sprung forward to embrace him. The prisoner folded his arms about his friend; but the surprise proved too much for him, and he sunk speechless on Rhinaldo's bosom. In a little time, however, he recovered himself.

"Gracious heaven!" exclaimed he, "to meet Rhinaldo in the place of my executioner." "Let us rid you," said Rhinaldo, "of these chains." The chains which secured him were fastened by a strong bolt round each leg. Rhinaldo thought that if his boots were cut off, the link would prove large enough to slip over his foot. He asked Gaspard for a knife, who went in search of one, but in ascending the stairs, found the dagger of Fabian, which had dropped from his girdle as he fell; with this he returned. Count Tancred's boots were slit down and taken off, but the link was smaller than they had supposed—it was necessary they should be unlocked or filed.

Gaspard then told Rhinaldo, that the key of the Count's fetters was probably in Fabian's pocket, which was immediately searched, and Count Tancred, whose impatience would only suffer them to unlock the link which fastened him to the stone, wrapt his chains round his arm, and followed his friend out of the dungeon. His mind was agitated by a most insatiable curiosity—he asked a thousand questions in a moment. "I will lead you,"—said Rhinaldo, "to one who will assist me in my detail—for, to say the truth, I am, at present, rather weary."

Rhinaldo was at this time accompanying his friend up the steps of the vault. "You look faint," said Count Tancred; ——"You bleed too, my friend!" They reached the vaulted chamber, where the Count was finally freed from his fetters.

"Here," said Rhinaldo, "lie your foes." Tancred surveyed the bodies. "Merciless barbarian!" said he, as he contemplated that of the Count;—"Why was not thy punishment reserved for me? But Rhinaldo," continued he, in a faltering voice, "there is——a——beauteous wretched victim——"

Rhinaldo threw himself into a chair. "I feel," said he, "too much embarrassed, by a slight wound I have received, to accompany you up stairs.—This person will conduct you where your question will be more efficaciously resolved; but stay—it will be proper, perhaps, to secure the fidelity of your guide—so saying, Rhinaldo pointed to the sword of the Count de St. Amand, which lay on the floor. "But you, my friend," said Tancred, taking up the sword,—"You want assistance."—"You will find my old servant, Rugiero, above," said Rhinaldo, "send him to me."

Count Tancred now quitted Rhinaldo, and, under the direction of Gaspard, sought the apartment of the lady. Rhinaldo had not been left many minutes in the vaulted chamber, before Rugiero attended him. He examined the wound in his thigh, and found it slight indeed; but by subsequent irritation much inflamed. He drest it as well as the little assistance he was enabled to procure on the spot would permit him, when Rhinaldo, addressing him with an air which marked the confidence he reposed in him, said, "It will be impossible for me to pursue my journey in this state—mark attentively the commands I am about to lay upon you—make with all speed towards the capital, and at the third house to the right, in the narrow street which leads from the little square to the back of the palace gardens, you will find my old serjeant, and your former comrade, Bernard Tilly; he will take care of your horse—remain in his house 'till night, and when you hear the palace clock strike twelve, repair to the high bridge——there you will find a man walking muffled up in his cloak, with his hat drawn over his eyes—accost this man immediately, and say to him, "*yes* or *no?*" If he should answer "*yes*," repair to me with all speed.—If "*no*," follow him without speaking, and whatsoever you may judge may be for my service, execute it suddenly and boldly. Know, Rugiero, that the task I impose on you requires presence of mind and intrepidity; but I have had sufficient experience of your heart and mind, to bid me rely with confidence on you. You will perhaps want money in the progress of the undertaking—take this ring."

Rhinaldo here presented a ring to Rugiero.—"Call on Ben Napthali, who lives to the west of the great square, and he will supply you, on sight of it, with whatever money you may want."

Rugiero, though he knew not what it was to disobey his master, and felt himself honored by the confidence reposed in him, yet could not help suggesting that he felt some uneasiness at leaving him in his present state——wounded, and in the house of his enemies. But Rhinaldo soothed his apprehensions, by telling him that Count Tancred was with him, and that there were, as he had learned, only three male domestics in the house.

Rugiero, after conducting his master up stairs, who found

Count Tancred and the lady in a more convenient apartment than that in which she had been confined, to which the women, who had been called to attend her, had had humanity enough to remove her, went to seek for his horse, and having found both his own and that of his master under the porch, from which they had not moved, he set off by the light of the dawn, which just now began to appear, in search of some place in which he might find provender for them: His eye soon directed him to a building, resembling a stable, which was in many places unroofed, but which still afforded a tolerable shelter. He led his horses gently in his hand, and opening the door, discovered that he had not been deceived. In this stable he found a man occupied in saddling a horse. This man started at seeing Rugiero, and let fall the saddle, which he was lifting to throw over the horse's back.

Rugiero clapped his hand to his sword, and the man seizing the horse hastily by the bridle, drew him, unsaddled as he was, out at an opposite door. Rugiero, encumbered with two horses, knew not readily what to do. In an instant, however, he quitted them both, and rushed on foot through the door at which this person had fled. He found the man already mounted on the bare back of the horse, who seemed to be possessed of much fire, for he sprung forward in a moment with considerable agility.—Rugiero sprung forward also, but in vain. The man pressed his horse eagerly, and, circling the house, gained the corner of the moat at which Rugiero and his master had passed, and driving his steed resolutely at it, passed it without accident, and fled with speed into the thickest of the forest.

Rugiero, at first, thought of pursuing the fugitive, and hastened back for his horse; but, upon a little reflection, he gave up this design. His horse was exhausted with fatigue, and the want of provender, while that of the fugitive was probably fresh. It would, besides, be almost impossible to trace him in a wild so trackless and deserted as the forest;

he therefore contented himself with searching the stables for provender, which, having obtained, he placed before his master's horse and his own, and returned once more into the house to acquaint Rhinaldo with the circumstance which had just occurred.

In passing the door, an impulse, which he could not resist, induced him first to turn into the vaulted chamber, and he there imagined he discovered cause of the singular circumstance which had just occurred. He found the body of the Count de St. Amand removed from the middle of the room, where he had left it, to a corner close under the window, which was opened to admit the light of the dawn, probably for the purpose of contemplating the face of the deceased.

He had now little doubt but that one of the servants had, during the period in which he conducted Rhinaldo up stairs, entered the vaulted chamber, and discovered the death of the Count St. Amand.

This circumstance, as he judged, was of extreme importance to the safety of his master, and he hastened to inform Rhinaldo of it, who gave him full credit for the fidelity of his attachment towards him, but continued to urge him strongly to hasten his departure.

Rugiero, therefore, returned to the stable, and his horse being somewhat refreshed, he led him to the draw-bridge, and letting it down, passed over it, directing his course towards that part of the forest from which he judged that his master and himself had deviated, when the storm had compelled them to seek refuge in the mansion.

CHAP. IV.

THE Countess St. Amand, for such, by the reproaches of the Count, Rhinaldo perceived her to be, was now much recovered from the recent indisposition which the horrors of the night had caused. Though she could not but feel deeply and awfully impressed by the singular events which had taken place, she did not affect any extraordinary degree of concern for the death of a man, whose cruel and ferocious disposition had rendered him the detestation of all who knew him; her health indeed seemed to have been impaired by the inhuman conduct of this barbarian towards her, and the roses had faded in her cheek. She was, however, notwithstanding this, extremely beautiful; and the benevolence of her heart was conspicuous in the gratitude which she did not cease to express towards her deliverer. The concern she felt at hearing of his wound, could scarcely be soothed by the tender attention of Tancred, nor by the repeated assurances of Rhinaldo himself, that the wound was trifling, and that he had a thorough confidence in the skill of his domestic, which he had in some similar instances previously experienced.

The day had now completely dawned, and the Countess proposed to Tancred and Rhinaldo, that they should take some repose after the fatigues they had undergone; but the intelligence which they had recently received from Rugiero, of the escape of the servant, was of too serious a nature to permit them, for the present, to enjoy a thought of repose; and anxious as they severally were to have the wonderful events of the night explained to them, they were compelled to delay the gratification of their curiosity, and consult together on the measures to be pursued in a moment so pregnant with danger to themselves.

Rugiero, in the mean time, pursued his journey with as much speed as possible, and arrived, without meeting any extraordinary adventure, at the capital. He reached the house of Bernard Tilly, and, having put up his horse, waited, not without anxiety, for the eventful hour of twelve. The clock from the neighbouring convent at length struck, and Rugiero snatching up his cloak and his sword, hastened towards the high bridge. He found, as he passed, the streets deserted. The inhabitants had all retired to bed—he gained the high bridge, and as he advanced towards the centre of it, he discovered a man wrapt in a cloak, walking with a slow and thoughtful pace towards him. This man passed Rugiero, without seeming to notice him; when Rugiero, according to his instructions, put to him the question,—"YES or NO?" The man answered immediately, "NO;" and wrapping his cloak about him, quickened his pace, and proceeded forward, without so much as looking at Rugiero.

Rugiero followed him through several winding streets, 'till he turned into a passage so narrow that it involved them in compleat darkness. Rugiero continued, however, to follow the man, 'till the passage opened into a kind of square, which appeared to be in a state of desolation. The ground was rough, uneven, and full of hillocks. Their path was interrupted by fragments of stone, bricks, and rubbish; and the stench which arose around them, betrayed it to be the residence of the meanest and most wretched inhabitants of the metropolis.

They at last reached a stone building, seemingly of very ancient structure, the entrance to which was a gothic door, so low that a moderate sized man must stoop considerably at entering it, and very narrow.

At this door the man tapped gently, and a small grated wicket in the middle of it was immediately unlocked.— Some words in a low voice passed—the door opened, as far as a chain, which was placed across it on the inside, would permit—and two men, with drawn daggers, appeared as centinels on the inside, Rugiero and his conductor were admitted—they passed under the chain, and the door was immediately closed.

They passed through a long winding passage, and up a narrow flight of stone stairs, at the top of which they tapped at a door, and were admitted into a large, gloomy, and almost unfurnished room, illuminated by a single lamp, which hung over a table.

Several men, whose persons could not, on account of the gloomy light which the lamp diffused, be very accurately distinguished, were walking about the room, conversing with each other. When Rugiero was admitted, his guide approached them, and having said something to them in a low voice, passed out of a door at the farther end of the room, and in a few minutes returned, accompanied by a gentleman with a taper in his hand, who advanced hastily towards Rugiero; but stopped short when he had approached near enough to distinguish him, and said, with signs of disappointment, "how is this? Is not your lord here?"

Rugiero, who knew him to be a young nobleman bound by the strictest ties of friendship to his lord, explained to him shortly the accident which had prevented Rhinaldo's arrival; but added, modestly, that whatever service they might think proper to employ him in, he hoped and trusted he should go through it with firmness.

"I do not doubt it," said the nobleman: "but your lord's counsel and conduct on a day like this——his absence affects us—it is, as it were, a limb lopped from our enterprise."

He then turned towards the remainder of the company, and entered into a long conversation with them.

Rugiero, by the light of the taper, which this gentleman had brought, added to that of the lamp, had an opportunity of viewing more distinctly the figures of these persons. They seemed all armed and accoutred for immediate service. The nobleman who addressed him, though not completely armed, had on his cuirasse, and other pieces, which were not sufficiently cumberous to prevent his acting on foot.

After having conversed for some time with the rest, this nobleman turned to Rugiero, and bade him follow him. They passed through the door at the end of the room, and arrived at a small chamber, in which there was a common truckle bed and two chairs.

"This," said the nobleman, smiling, "is my apartment. But come," added he, "let us lose no time." He passed through this apartment, and descending by a staircase on the other side of it, entered a room, in which were several armed men, some walking, some sitting down, and others lying on benches. Several pieces of armour hung round the walls, and swords and pikes seemed scattered carelessly about.

"Come, my friends," said the nobleman, as he entered— "our hour is arrived;" twelve of them then took up their arms, and the nobleman, followed by Rugiero, led them to the gate at which the latter had entered, which was opened at their approach.

They passed over the ruins, and keeping the most profound silence, gained the new bridge. They did not pass over it, but passing down on one side of the river, discovered at no great distance a boat, in which sate two men.

These men arose at their approach, and the nobleman having said something to them, addressed Rugiero as follows:——

"I must now leave you, as my presence is demanded elsewhere. These men will conduct you to the gardens at the back of the palace—there, if fortune befriends us, you will find the princess Isabel. This will prove an eventful night. Your task will probably require fortitude and presence of mind. If you have the good fortune to effect the escape of the princess, convey her with all speed to the place whence we now came."

Saying this, the nobleman, with four of his comrades, departed, leaving Rugiero with the rest, who immediately embarked in the boat prepared for them. Rugiero now perceived that the two men in the boat were also armed.

CHAP. V.

THEY dropped silently down with the tide, rowing as gently as possible, lest the dashing of their oars, amid the stillness of the night, should create some alarm.

When they arrived at the back of the palace gardens, which opened by a beautiful and lofty terrace towards the river. They were surprised by the sound of many voices, and could faintly discover several persons moving on the terrace. They now took in their oars entirely, and as the tide carried them slowly opposite the terrace, preserved the most profound silence.—They did not, however, execute this so successfully, as not to be perceived. They were challenged from the terrace, and ordered to bring to. In spite, however, of this order, they still continued to drop down with the tide, about the middle of the channel, when they were alarmed by the report of an arquebusse, evidently levelled at them; the shot, however, probably went over their heads, as they did not perceive any effect from it. They now thought it necessary again to ply their oars, which they did with some effect, but remitted their labour upon hearing a bugle sound in the garden, at the call of which the soldiers, whom they had seen upon the terrace, suddenly disappeared, and left the gardens wrapt in total silence.

Rugiero, upon this, resolved to land there, and ordering the boat to pull in gently towards the terrace, he threw a ladder of ropes, with which the boatmen were purposely provided, over the parapet; but the breadth of the wall prevented the grapplings, which were fixed to the end of the ladder, taking hold. They then pushed the boat towards a large flight of stone stairs, which descended from a magnificent portico about the centre of the terrace, and entangling their grapplings with some wrought iron which united the gateway with the parapet, Rugiero ascended the ladder, and was followed by the whole of his party, except the two persons he had found in the boat, who still remained to take care of it. They paced silently along the terrace, and sought the most retired part of the garden, intending to conceal themselves in the bowers with which it abounded.

They had not proceeded far, before they discovered two women, who passed swiftly between the trees. Terror seemed to lend them wings. Rugiero and his party had scarcely time to observe them, before they saw their progress impeded by a party of armed men, whose leader, advancing towards the women, laid hold on the foremost of them by the arm, while his party surrounded them.

Rugiero, who immediately conjectured that this must be the Lady Isabel, ordered his men to stand to their arms, and advanced resolutely towards them. The women shrieked, and Rugiero heard the leader of the opposite band exclaim, "It is the Lady Isabel——secure her."

Upon hearing this, Rugiero rushed on him, and was resolutely seconded by his men, one of whom gently led the women towards the terrace, while the rest, placing their backs towards them, in a firm phalanx, covered the retreat. In this manner they gained the terrace; but the exclamations of the opposite party, who called loudly for assistance, and the clashing of their swords, had by this time so far increased the number of their enemies, that though they had gained the portico at which the ladder was suspended, they found themselves so pressed, that they began to give up every hope of escape. They had found means, however, with the assistance of the men below, to convey the two women safely to the boat, and calling to those below to push off, had no thoughts but of selling their lives as dearly as possible— when the attention of the foe was suddenly diverted by a violent attack on the gate of the portico, and in an instant

Rugiero found his little forlorn party succoured by a strong reinforcement, who mounted the terrace by the rope ladder, which still hung suspended to the iron work of the portico.

The gate in a short time was opened by assistance from the inside, and a considerable party, who had disembarked from boats which lay moored to the staircase below, rushed at once into the garden. The enemy found it in vain to contend longer, and made a precipitate retreat, in which they were closely pressed by the party which had just arrived.

Rugiero, who had luckily (though very hardly pressed) escaped without a wound, was now preparing to descend the ladder, in order to secure the retreat of the Lady Isabel, when he was accosted by a person belonging to the party just entered, who, calling him by his name, asked him, if the lady was safe?

Rugiero knew this person immediately to be the nobleman he had so lately quitted, and his surprise at this unexpected meeting kept him for a moment silent.

"We have been betrayed," added this nobleman. "Our troops have met with a warm reception in the square, and I have embarked with this reserve to try whether this part of the palace would not prove less impregnable than the front; but where," continued he, "is the lady Isabel?"

Rugiero told him that she was in the boat below, and he descended immediately by the ladder. In about five minutes he returned. "Rugiero," said he, "we have been deceived.— The lady in the boat is not the Lady Isabel; she is, however, a lady, in whose welfare I interest myself much. The duty of the moment will not permit me to stay——the Lady Isabel is confined in her chamber in the first story on the left front of the western tower. I will leave a trusty few for the guard of the boat, and with thirty more, whom I will spare to reinforce your detachment, you must attempt to rescue the lady." Having remained just long enough to effect this arrangement, the nobleman hastened towards the palace.

Rugiero now took the command of the men who were delivered to him by the nobleman, and sought the western tower. He perceived the window on the left front—it was about the height of two pikes from the ground, and grated with iron—he perceived that the chamber within was lighted up; he had taken the precaution to bring from the boat the ladder of ropes; he tied two pikes together, and, hoisting the ladder, fixed the grapplings to the bars of the windows and ascended. The light in the chamber grew every moment more and more vivid. What were the horrors which Rugiero felt when, upon gaining the window, he perceived the furniture and hangings of the chamber enveloped in flames.

He had scarcely time to reflect on this dreadful spectacle, before he heard the clashing of swords, and perceived that his men were attacked below.—The garden was again in tumult, and the party which had lately landed were compelled to retreat to their boats, which they did in much confusion.

Rugiero's guard stood boldly on their defence, but were presently overpowered by numbers, and compelled to seek their safety with the rest. In this confusion Rugiero stood supported by the gratings of the window, 'till the flames began to crack the panes of the casement, and his post was become too hot to be longer tenable. He now began to descend, when, either from the melting of the solder, through the increasing heat of the walls, or from the rottenness of the iron-work itself, the grating gave way, and Rugiero fell to the ground.

He lay, for some time, stunned by his fall, and upon recovering himself, found that the tumult in the garden had in a great measure subsided. He had luckily received no material damage from this accident, and now thought of effecting his escape; but reflecting for a moment on his situation, he judged it useless to proceed towards the terrace, as the boats had probably by this time quitted the shore.

As he walked slowly forwards, doubtful what he should do, he perceived before him the body of a man, who had probably been slain in the late skirmish, and who was drest in the habit of the king's guard.

Rugiero hesitated not a moment, but stripping him of his hat, his buff coat, and bandelier, and placing his arquebusse on his shoulder, he fell in with a party who were in an irregular manner retiring towards the palace, and insinuating himself among them, soon gained the great square in the front of the building.

He here found most of the troops in the city drawn up, and under arms, while a party were employed in extinguishing the fire which had filled his mind with so much horror.

Musing on the dreadful fate which had probably attended the unfortunate lady, for whose sake solely he seemed to have been commanded on his present service, and shuddering at the bare idea of communicating to his lord intelligence so pregnant with calamity, he quitted the square, unperceived by some sentries who were posted at the different avenues, but who were employed in drinking, and gained the high bridge. From the high bridge, he strove to retrace his former steps towards the spot on which he had first seen the noble friend of his lord. In this he succeeded; but, on his arrival, he had fresh cause for astonishment and alarm. He saw the ruins almost covered with dead bodies—a large party of the king's troops were still there under arms—the building, at the little door of which he had been so cautiously admitted, was smoking in ruins, and, opposite to it, were placed two small pieces of artillery. In short, there was every appearance that this house had been defended to the last extremity.

Rugiero retired with a melancholy step from this scene of slaughter, and regaining the house of Bernard Tilly, he mounted his horse, and prepared to convey to his master the heavy and heart-breaking intelligence with which he felt his mind oppressed. At the eastern gate, through which it was necessary that he should attempt his escape, he judged that he should not be able to pass without some difficulty.—He resolved, however, to depend on the coat he wore, and the tale he should be able to fabricate, in all probability this would scarcely have succeeded; but he was not put to the trial—he found the post deserted—the guard had been recently attacked, and the gate forced—he now took the road towards the place where he had left Rhinaldo.

CHAP. VI.

R UGIERO rode on, wrapt in mournful mediation, 'till he came to the skirts of a wood. As he entered the hollow way, which led through this wood, he heard a noise of the galloping of horses at a distance behind him. He turned round, and perceived a troop of horsemen, at the distance of about a quarter of a mile, pressing with all their speed towards him.

As he did not think it prudent to encounter these men, he put his horse forward, and perceiving a narrow path winding through the thicket on his right hand, he turned his horse into it, and giving him the spur, and defending his face as well as he could with his hand, he speedily lost sight of the road. He pursued the path, which became gradually more open, 'till thinking himself well concealed from the horsemen, whose approach had alarmed him, he paused. He had the satisfaction to hear them pass along the road, without attempting to turn out of it. He then thought of returning the way he came, but perceived the thicket so deeply entangled, that he was compelled to pursue the path strait forward.

It extended gradually, as he proceeded, 'till it opened into a green sward, shaped like a little amphitheatre, and surrounded, on all sides, by the wood. As he entered this place, he perceived the back of a man, who was gliding through the trees at the other end of it. He stopped his horse when he perceived this, and, as he was meditating on the path he should pursue, he was surrounded by four men, who rushed out of the surrounding thickets so suddenly, that they had seized upon his bridle and sword before he was aware of their approach.

They told him he was their prisoner, and, bidding him dismount, tied his hands behind him, and led him thro' the thickest of the underwood,—his horse being conducted by one of them slowly behind. After a toilsome walk of some length, their path being interrupted by briars and matted weeds, and the hands of his conductors employed in removing the branches by which they were perpetually interrupted. They arrived at the foot of a rock, gradually sloping from a prodigious height, crowned on the summit with lofty and majestic pines, and clad to the very foot with brush wood, intermingled with small dwarf trees.

Beneath this rock were some cabins, freshly constructed with the branches of trees, and one indeed scarcely yet begun. Several persons were employed in the labour of rearing them, whose arms lay by them.

Rugiero was conducted to the largest of the huts, which was built so as to form a kind of vestibule to a cave, which seemed to have been scooped by nature in the solid rock. From this hut a person advanced to meet him, who seemed, as he could collect from the behaviour of the rest, vested with some authority.

The men who had seized Rugiero informed this person, that being detached for forage, they had fallen in with the prisoner as he was attempting to discover their retreat, and, as was beyond all doubt confirmed by his appearance, in order to betray it to the king.

The person whom they addressed, turning to Rugiero, asked him how he came into that situation. "But," added he, "his garb is evidence enough of his intention—we must teach him, that despair has rendered all attempts against us dangerous—let him be conveyed aside, and well guarded—we will speedily determine on his fate." Rugiero begged to be heard; but the person who had given these orders turning his back upon him, the men who had him in custody were about to convey him away, when he perceived an officer of a superior presence approach.

This officer held by the hand a lady, plainly but hand-somely drest. What was the satisfaction of Rugiero, when he discovered in him the very nobleman under whose auspices he had conducted the business of the preceding evening.

The nobleman to whom his case was referred, knew him immediately; ordered him to be unbound, and taking him into the cave, asked him by what singular fortune he had escaped from the calamities which attended the unfortunate events of the night.

The apartment in the cave was lofty and spacious. It received a degree of light, just sufficient to render it habitable, by an oblique perforation in the roof, which joined to the surface of the rock at some considerable height above the entrance. In this apartment, which had in former times been the residence of a hermit, were three chairs and a table, carved rudely in wood, and seemingly very old. At the end was a rude altar, formed in the solid rock, having a crucifix carved with some ingenuity over it; and in the corner of the cave lay a small bedstead of wood, which was covered with fearn, newly gathered.

Rugiero related to the young nobleman, with horror in his countenance, the dreadful object which encountered him at Lady Isabel's window; and the circumstances which attended his escape.

"Heaven be praised!" said this nobleman, who was called Count Anselmo;—"all then is yet well. This lady," said he, turning towards the lady, whom he held by the hand, "is indebted to you for her escape last night. You mistook her for the Lady Isabel, to whom indeed she is nearly related. Upon the ill success of our last attempt, I had the good fortune to reach the boat in which you left this lady, and the equally good fortune to fall down the river under the very walls of the fort, which guards the entrance of the city, unperceived. We have trembled for the fate of the Lady Isabel, who, upon the discovery of our plot, was closely confined. But all, I trust, is yet well. Rugiero," continued he, "you must undertake another journey to the city, for your master's service; but, as the alarm is spread, it will be necessary for you to disguise yourself. Where," said he, speaking to one of his attendants, "is the woodman, whose guests we are?"

A poor fellow was presently called to him, who was employed in finishing one of the cabins, but who was closely watched, lest he should make his escape.

"You had better," said Anselmo to Rugiero, "change dresses with this fellow. In his garb, and driving the sorry beast on which he loads his faggots, you may easily gain admittance into the city."

To this proposal Rugiero immediately consented. He disguised himself like a peasant, and, loading an ass belonging to the woodman with faggots, he waited the commands of Anselmo.

"When you have gained the city," said the Count, "repair to ——" here he paused——"Hath your lord," said he, "given you any order to receive money in the city?"

Rugiero produced the ring he had received from Rhinaldo.

"All is right," continued the Count. "Ask of Ben Naphthali a thousand crowns in gold; when you have got it, wait patiently 'till the clock strikes nine; repair then to the colonade in the front of the town-house, where, during the day, the merchants assemble. You will there find the person whom you saw on the high bridge; but be extremely cautious how you act. Your life, and the welfare of your lord, will perhaps depend on your care.—Do not, therefore, whomsoever you may see there, address him; but place yourself with your back against the fifth pillar of the colonade from the right. If the person, seeing you in that situation, should ask you the question you formerly asked, "*yes* or *no*," he is your man. Deliver to him the thousand crowns, and attend to the orders he will give you—do not, however, loiter long in the streets after this interview, as the city patrole will soon afterwards mount guard."

Rugiero, armed with these instructions, soon departed; but fearing, not withstanding his disguise, an examination at the city gates, he adopted the precaution of sewing the ring within the lining of his pack saddle. Nor did this care prove needless—at the gates he underwent a strict search; but having taken great care that nothing about him should convey the slightest suspicion of his being in any degree superiour to the rank of the peasant he appeared, they suffered him to pass.

As soon as he had conveyed his load of faggots to a wretched inn, to which the woodmen usually restored, he prepared himself to execute the orders of Count Anselmo. He procured the money of Ben Naphthali, and repaired, when the clock stuck nine, to the place appointed. He had scarcely placed himself against the pillar, when the man he had formerly seen walked slowly by him, so close as to brush him with his cloak. After a short time he returned, and perceiving nobody near, addressed him in the words he had been taught to expect.

Upon this, Rugiero drew a canvass bag from his breast, in which were contained the thousand crowns he had received from Naphthali, and gave them to the stranger, who, putting them under his cloak, told him to be in the same spot exactly in six hours—but to take particular care, if possible, to avoid the patrole.

Rugiero returned to his miserable inn, and throwing

himself on a truckle bed, waited with impatience the expiration of the six hours. The clock at length struck three—he arose, and hastened towards the place of appointment. He had not proceeded many paces before, at the corner of a street, he met the patrole. He started aside, to avoid the serjeant, whose suspicions were so far aroused by this circumstance, that he immediately sprung forward, and seized him by the collar. He was soon surrounded, and after a few questions taken into custody, and marched towards the guard-house.

He had not proceeded far beyond the town-house, when the guard, in whose custody he was, were encountered by another party. As soon as these parties came close to each other, they halted, which they had scarcely done, when a man springing forward from the midst of the party which had just arrived, seized Rugiero by the collar, and said to the commander of the detachment he was with, "This is the traitor—this is the very man we are in search of—I charge you seize him."

The commander, upon these words, advanced towards Rugiero, gave him into the custody of his own party, after a few words had passed between him and the serjeant of the other detachment, when the parties separated, each returning the way they came.

The astonishment of Rugiero kept him perfectly silent under this accusation; nor was that astonishment lessened, by his perceiving that the person accusing him was the very man to whom he had so lately delivered the thousand crowns, and who had promised to meet him.

He was now convinced that he was betrayed, and that his own life, and the dearest interests of his lord, must fall a sacrifice to his ill fortune. Yet how it had occurred he could not divine.—Wrapt in these melancholy reflections, he walked on 'till they came to the remains of the old palace, a building which had long been converted into a prison, for which use one would have thought, from its appearance, it had been originally designed.

In an outward apartment belonging to this place, the guard which had conducted Rugiero hither halted, and deposited their arms; and this faithful servant was ordered to follow the commander of the party, who led him into a dark and intricate passage, while the person who had preferred the accusation against him kept warily behind him. They passed through many strong doors, of which the commander possessed the keys. At length they descended by the winding staircase of a turret, and passing a long and narrow arched vault, lighted by two dim lamps, began to ascend in the same manner. After ascending for some time, the guide halted, and, opening a door, introduced Rugiero to a small strong square room, which seemed to admit the light in the day by one small casement, opened in a wall of immense thickness. In short, it seemed a place of confinement for prisoners of a better order, who were not destined to be very rigidly dealt with.

In this room, at a table, on which burned two tapers, sat a young man, plainly drest, who seemed, as it appeared to Rugiero upon entering, in the act of painting his face by a looking-glass which stood on the table; while another person, of about his own stature, stood at his elbow, assisting him in the employment.

Such an employment, in such a situation, could not fail to strike Rugiero. The young man arose suddenly upon their entrance, and, taking his cloak and hat from his attendant, seemed to await their orders.

Rugiero had now an opportunity of viewing him. He seemed very young, of an elegant form, and brown complexion, his hair very much overshadowed his face, and, as well as his eyebrows, was remarkably dark.

Rugiero's guide accosted him respectfully, and, taking off his hat, told him that the *time was come*. The young man's servant upon this took up a small cloak bag, which was delivered to Rugiero, and attended his master, who followed the conductor to the guard room. The escort who had conducted Rugiero to this place, resumed their arms, and proceeded towards the gate of the city, at which Rugiero had entered, but halted within about forty paces of it, when the commander, apologizing for the necessity he was under, ordered the young man and his servant to be bound together. The same ceremony was performed on Rugiero and his accuser, who were, to his surprise, bound arm to arm.

When they arrived at the gate, the commander asked for the serjeant of the guard, and told him he was conducting some prisoners to a castle, which he named, at no great distance. He then gave him the word of the night. The gate was opened, the drawbridge let down, and the detachment soon saw themselves clear of the city.

CHAP. VII.

THE leaders of this little party no sooner found themselves out of sight of the gates, than they unbound the four prisoners, and striking out of the road, pursued their march through a hollow way, which in a few hours led them to the skirts of a forest.

During this march, Rugiero found himself treated with much respect by the person who commanded the detachment, and the man to whom he had delivered the thousand crowns.—The latter apologized to him for the manner in which he had been treated; but told him, that when he found him unfortunately in the custody of the other escort, he perceived there was no other mode of extricating him, than that of preferring the accusation, upon which he had been delivered up. Upon the arrival of the detachment at the skirts of this forest, they were met by a party of horse, at the head of which Rugiero saw the Count Anselmo. This nobleman rode immediately up to the detachment, and dismounting from his horse, addressed himself most respectfully to the young man who had accompanied them from the prison, and insisted upon his riding during the rest of the journey. This offer the young man, who seemed much exhausted with fatigue, accepted, with many thanks, and was helped by the Count into the saddle. His servant was likewise accommodated with the charger of one of the troopers, and the party pursued their march 'till they arrived, by a very narrow path, which would just admit a single horse, at the spot from which Rugiero had been detached on the preceding day.

On their arrival, the Count conducted the young man and his attendant into the cave, and ordered Rugiero to follow.

On his entrance to the cave, he was surprized to see the lady, whom he had left with the Count, rise from her seat, and embrace the young man with ardour—but his surprise was quickly alleviated by the Count, who said to him, "Rugiero, I may now congratulate you on your Lord's approaching happiness. This," added he, taking the young man by the hand, "is the Princess Isabel."

Rugiero dropped on one knee, and the lady stretching out her hand to raise him, he pressed it respectfully to his lips.

"Where," said she to Rugiero, "is your Lord? How came he absent at a time like this? Is he safe? Is he well?"

"He is safe, Madam," said Rugiero; "and a few hours will conduct me to him."

"Why is he not here?" said she.

Anselmo, to whom Rugiero had disclosed the cause of Rhinaldo's absence, then told her that an accident had prevented the Count's attendance, but that she should see him on the next day.

"My dear Cousin Ellenor," said the Princess, turning to her, and embracing her with much affection, "I did not think

I should ever see you again. Blessed be heaven for this interview!"

"To what propitious fortune," said the other lady, returning her embrace with equal ardour, "am I indebted for this
happiness?"

"I scarcely," said the Princess, "know myself. You remember, my dear Cousin, that, on the day preceding that evening,
when it was agreed that I should attempt my escape from
the detested addresses of the son of the Count St. Amand, I
was closely confined to my chamber. The cause of that confinement was the rumour of a plot to restore my father to his
throne. Of my escape I know little. I was alarmed by the cry
of fire. I heard a confused noise at my door, which was suddenly opened. I was conveyed, with my faithful Barbara, to a
room in the old palace, whither, late last night, the disguises
in which we now appear were conveyed to us. Ah! Count
Anselmo," continued the Princess, "Tell me, I intreat you,
my father! is he safe?"

"He is, Madam," said Anselmo; "it was not thought proper,
'till this effort was made, to draw him from his retirement.
The project of making ourselves masters of the person of
your uncle, and thus securing the capital, was entrusted but
to few. Rhinaldo was among them. You will, I know, pardon
him, that he did not confide to you the whole of our project.
Such a confidence he knew, from the delicacy of your situation, could alone be attended with pain, anxiety, and eventually, perhaps, with danger to your person. As Rhinaldo could
not appear in the capital with safety, it was resolved that he
should not join us 'till our project was ripe for execution, and
that then he should enter the town privately, and meet one
of our party at a place appointed. If any thing had happened
to disconcert our measures, at a word given by the person
appointed to meet him, Rhinaldo was to take horse and fly to
bring up some troops, who are collected on the frontiers; if
nothing had happened, he was to join us. Rugiero attended us

in his place, and, receiving the word intended for his lord, was conducted to us, for we did not then suspect, what we afterwards proved, that our plot had been discovered. As to your own escape, it was effected by a serjeant of Astolpho's guard, who had formerly served your father, and was attached to us. He had been informed of your confinement, and projected, with an officer of our party, the plan for your escape, which was speedily communicated to me. In the midst of the confusion, which occurred in the palace, he contrived to set fire to the chamber adjoining to yours, and prevailing on the guard, which was set over you, to open your doors, he entered with his own men, and, under pretence of conveying you to your uncle, lodged you in the old palace. But if you wish to learn the story from his own mouth, here he is."

At that instant the commander of the party, which had escorted Isabel to this retirement, entered.

Isabel arose. "At least," said she, "I ought to express my obligations to him." She now began to thank the serjeant for his conduct—when he interrupted her suddenly.

"Lady," said he, "this is no time for compliments. Heaven grant that you may yet be in safety."

"My Lord," said he to the Count, "your scouts bring us but scurvy intelligence. Several soldiers have been discovered making through the thickest of the wood in different parts, and there is reason to think we are discovered."

Alarmed at this intelligence, Anselmo arose, and walked hastily towards the mouth of the cave. He had scarcely reached it, when a horseman, who had been out to reconnoitre, brushed suddenly thro' the winding path in the wood, by which Anselmo had conducted Isabel to the cave, and riding hastily up to the Count, told him, that from an eminence he had discerned a large party, consisting both of infantry and cavalry, marching towards the skirts of the forest, and that a detachment of light troops were already upon the scout in the wood.

There was not now much time for debate. It was suddenly resolved that Anselmo, with a chosen party, mounted on the best horses they had, and carrying with them the little stock of provisions which they had already been enabled to procure, consisting chiefly of the flesh of some wild goats, should immediately retire thro' the forest, in order either to gain some station where their friends were assembled, or to fall in with the troops, which they hoped were already on their march from the frontiers; while Rugiero and the sergeant should form a kind of rear guard with the foot to cover their retreat, and check the enemy's horse, who could alone hope to overtake them.

This check they had no doubt they could effectually give, favoured as they were by the inaccessible nature of the ground, and their resolve was no sooner formed than executed. Isabel, her Cousin, and servant, were mounted, and, escorted by Count Anselmo and a chosen party of horse, filed through the narrow path; Rugiero and the sergeant, with a party of foot, having first reconnoitered it, and secured the outlet, which opened into a hollow way leading to the deepest recesses of the forest.

Our fugitives had not long gained this road, when Rugiero perceived a small detachment of horse advancing from the opposite part of the road which led towards the city. Upon their approach, he threw his party into the woods on each side of the road, who made such use of their fire arms and arrows, that the horsemen finding them effectually secured from their attacks by the thickness of the wood, soon judged it prudent to retreat, and give up any farther pursuit 'till their infantry should arrive. During this time, Rugiero and his party gradually retreated after the Count, and had soon the satisfaction to find themselves wholly unmolested by their enemies.

They pushed forward with as much speed as they were able to make, 'till the shades of night, which fell heavily and deeply over the forest, in some measure arrested their progress. They were then compelled to proceed at a slower pace, for which they, however, felt somewhat consoled, by the reflection that their pursuers, if they were yet pursued, were equally impeded by the cause which obstructed them. The night now grew darker, and, amidst the gloom which was occasioned by the thick and lofty branches of the trees, they found it extremely difficult to discern the path before them, in which they were alone guided by the deep and rugged banks which arose on each side.

The wind now arose, and whistled hollow through the trees—the gloom seemed redoubled—the rain began to rattle amidst the trees—and the thunder to roll at a distance—while the howling of the wolves on every side of them filled the little party with dismay.

They knew the ferocity of these animals, with multitudes of which this forest abounded; and the darkness of the night rendered them liable to unforeseen attacks from every side.

While they were in this situation, keeping as close together as possible, through the dread they entertained of these voracious animals, they perceived a distant light glimmering through a vista in the forest, and determined, after a short deliberation, to make towards it, and procure, if possible, some shelter 'till the storm should subside.

It is true, that, by such a step, they subjected themselves to a discovery, or rendered their march liable to be traced, if the house from which the light proceeded should prove the mansion of some person inimical to their cause; but the fatigue and terrors of the female companions of his flight, and indeed their seeming inability to proceed farther, induced Anselmo to run all hazards, and turning towards the place whence the light they had discerned diffused its beams, they found themselves in a short time close to the walls of a spacious and stately castle.

It was here resolved that, as their numbers might create

suspicion, Rugiero, who was not so well known as the Count, and consequently was not so liable to detection, should, with the Lady Isabel, her Cousin, and attendants, demand admittance, and shelter from the storm, while the remainder of the party waited without, and sought protection from the boisterous inclemency of the night, in some of the outhouses of the Castle.

This they might easily do without detection, for though this Castle was large and stately, it was a place of no great strength. The situation did not admit of its being moated, and its outward defence was a wall of no considerable height.

Rugiero then, with Isabel and her fair companions, while the rest of the party stood aloof, shrouded by the darkness of the night, applied for admittance. He had slung round him a bugle horn, which Anselmo had given him, with orders, in case he found himself in danger, to sound an alarm. The apparel of Isabel and her companion was plain and neat, and Ellenor was covered with her veil. After some time the gate was opened, and Rugiero begged for shelter 'till the storm should pass over.

He said that his party had been attacked by the wolves, in passing the forest, and that they had been compelled, in order to save their own lives, to leave their horses a prey to those ravenous animals. After relating this story, they were, upon a short deliberation, admitted through the court into a lofty and spacious hall, hung round with armour.

The whole of the family seemed to have retired to rest, except a few servants, who were standing round a fire, to which Rugiero and his party advanced, in order to dry their cloaths. After some little time, the servants were summoned to attend their lord, who was preparing to retire for the night.

Rugiero and the Princess had waited but a few minutes, before they perceived the door of a room open, and two of the servants, who had just left them, descend by a few steps into the hall, bearing each a taper in his hand.

They were followed by a gentleman dressed in deep mourning, who advancing towards Rugiero and his companions, surveyed them with scrutinizing eyes; but what were the feelings of Isabel, when in this person she discovered the man with whose abhorred addresses she had been so much persecuted—the Count Rhodolpho, the son of the Count St. Amand.

Rhodolpho, after he had asked some questions of Rugiero, advanced towards her. She was sinking with terror—he looked at her, but, to all appearance, did not recollect her, for he passed on to her Cousin Ellenor, whom he desired to lift her veil. What were the sensations of Isabel at this request! She knew that Rhodolpho was perfectly acquainted with her Cousin.—Ellenor, who likewise knew him, hesitated and trembled. He intimated his desire with the tone of a man who would be obeyed.

Isabel, instinctively, caught hold of the horn which hung by Rugiero's side, and raised it to her mouth; but before her lips could reach it, overcome by her sensations, she fainted and fell senseless on the floor.

This circumstance called off the attention of Rhodolpho, who no longer persisted in his demand, but leaving Isabel, whose accident he imputed to fatigue, to the care of his servants, retired.

He had scarcely turned his back, when Ellenor, forgetting all precaution at beholding her Cousin's situation, threw off her veil, and flew to the lady Isabel's assistance.

Of the servants who had attended Rhodolpho into the hall, two had remained behind. One of them was a shrewd fellow, whose subtilty and address had recommended him much to the favour of his lord.

The appearance of Isabel and her companion had struck him, as bearing in it something peculiar. The circumstance of her seizing the bugle, which hung at Rugiero's side, and attempting to sound it, had not passed unnoticed; and the beauty of Ellenor so ill according with the situation in which she appeared, convinced him that some mystery attended the arrival of these people at the Castle.

Impressed with this idea, while Rugiero, assisted by Ellenor, Barbara, and the other servant, was occupied in the recovery of Isabel, he stole away to his lord, and communicated to him all he had observed.

Rhodolpho, aroused by this intelligence, quitted his apartment, and returned to the hall, where he unluckily arrived, unseen by any one, before Ellenor had replaced her veil.

"Lady Ellenor!" exclaimed Rhodolpho, starting back. He looked alternately at her and Isabel, who was still sitting in the chair. The efforts used to recover her had disordered her dress——some false hair which she wore was displaced——the water sprinkled in her face had removed some of the paint which she had used to give a brown and manly hue to her complexion.

Rhodolpho looked stedfastly at her. He clasped his hands together; and raising them in a transport, exclaimed, "by all that's sacred, this was above my hopes! The Princess Isabel! At last, Madam, you are mine—nor is it in the power of heaven or earth to redeem you."

The arrival of all she had dreaded roused those spirits in the Princess which her fears had dissipated. She arose, and waving her hand, said to Rhodolpho, with an air of dignity,—"My Lord, I will remain no longer here—let me pass."

"See that no one escapes," said Rhodolpho to his servants. "Ladies," continued he, with a sneer,—"you must be content with my inhospitable roof to-night."

"Not so, my Lord," said Rugiero, firmly. "Since this is the case, we must trust again to the inclement elements;" and taking Isabel in one hand, and Ellenor in the other, he conducted them towards the door.

"On your lives, let no one pass," said Rhodolpho to his servants, who advanced towards the door.

Rugiero now quitting the hands of the ladies, drew his sword, and said, in a determined tone, "The man who attempts to obstruct our passage, dies."

Isabel, Barbara, and Ellenor, now ran towards the door, while Rugiero, still facing Rhodolpho and his servants, kept them at bay.

"Ring the alarm bell," cried Rhodolpho; and the servants flew different ways to arouse the sleepy inhabitants of the Castle.

Rugiero, finding himself freed from the unequal attacks of his foes, took advantage of this breathing time, and, applying his bugle horn to his mouth, sounded a charge, while the delicate and trembling hands of his companions were applied, with unskilful haste, to the massy bolts and bars of the door.

The active alarms of the servants soon brought assistance to their lord.

Rugiero found his assailants increase. He had repeatedly sounded his horn, when, to his extreme joy, he heard his friends on the outside of the door, which Isabel and her companions had at length contrived to unbar.

Count Anselmo, and his party, now rushed in, and giving a sudden check to the assailants of Rugiero, bore away the Princess, her Cousin, and companion. By this time, however, the hall was full of men, for Rhodolpho had quartered his company of men at arms (which his father's interest had obtained for him) at his Castle that night, with intent to join the king on the next day. They rushed out in pursuit of the fugitives, and as they exceeded Anselmo's little band considerably in numbers, the latter were compelled to seek refuge in the darkness of the night, and the thickness and obscurity of the tangled forest. Pressed by a formidable enemy, close at their heels, they knew not which course to take, but dispersed in different bodies, and sought their safety in flight.

Anselmo, who would not quit his mistress and her lovely

Cousin, found himself in a few minutes unaccompanied by any man of his party, except Rugiero. He sought the place where he had left his horses, and, with the assistance of Rugiero, having mounted his little female band as well as he could, they took the first path which led from the Castle, and pressing forward with all the speed they could make, soon found themselves free from the noise of their pursuers.

CHAP. VIII.

ANSELMO and his fair companions had travelled for some time, Rugiero purposely keeping behind, that, if any pursuit should be made after them, he might give early intelligence of it,—when the horse on which this brave and faithful servant was mounted fell suddenly with him.

Rugiero readily extricated himself from him, but notwithstanding every effort he could make, in vain attempted to raise this worn-out animal, whose strength was wholly exhausted. After endeavouring, without success, to make the Count, who was at some distance before him, acquainted with his disaster, for the roaring of the storm compleatly drowned his exclamations, he resolved to sit under a tree, close to the spot where his horse lay, and wait the approach of day with patience.

In the mean time, Count Anselmo, with the lady Ellenor, the Princess Isabel, and her companion, proceeded onward, unconscious of the fate of Rugiero. At last, however, hearing no longer the sound of his horse's feet, they stopped to listen—but they listened in vain. The howling of the wind was the only noise which saluted their ears. They knew not what to conjecture. Every idea they could form of the fate of Rugiero seemed pregnant with danger to themselves. They were at length, after a long period passed in painful and fruitless expectation, compelled to pursue their journey without him, which they did in a cheerless and melancholy silence, each of them brooding over ideas which they were almost afraid to communicate to the others.

They were journeying in this manner, when they came to a more open part of the forest, a large and dark object before them, which they were soon convinced was, as indeed it proved, a house. Somewhat revived at this prospect, they pushed forward, and speedily arrived at an old and ruined mansion.

In this ancient and dismantled dwelling, they perceived no signs of inhabitants. They judged it on that account a more proper shelter for the night; and though the Princess and her female companions were not unimpressed by terrors from the awfulness of the scene, they passed a crazy draw-bridge, and, crossing a court-yard, reached the door of the house, which Anselmo, dismounting, presently opened.

When he had opened it, he listened, but could hear nothing. He was the more convinced, by this circumstance, that the house was uninhabited, and prevailed, after much intreaty, on his timid companions to leave their horses, (which he fastened together) and enter the mansion with him.

The lightning, which had not as yet ceased to play around them, shooting through a large gothic window, displayed to them an old unfurnished hall. They found that the rain beat in near the spot where they stood, and the wind swept through the various avenues of this uncomfortable asylum. As they were much incommoded in this situation, Anselmo proposed that they should seek a better shelter; and after some opposition, his friends clinging close around him, proceeded across the hall, and descending by a few steps, found himself in a warmer station. He now began to trace his new apartment by the walls, and soon perceived, by the style of the furniture, and the extent of the fire-place, that he had reached the kitchen of this mansion.

In pursuing his discovery, he soon found out that this part of the mansion could not have been long uninhabited, and began to entertain hopes, if he could, by accident, procure any implement with which he might strike a light, of rendering their asylum less comfortless for the remainder of the time which they should be compelled pass in it.

His search was not unsuccessful, and it became apparent, to demonstration, that the house could not have been long forsaken. He found the implements he sought, and discovering some straw and faggots in a recess at no great distance from the fire-place, he kindled a fire, and easily prevailed on his shivering friends to draw round it.

It was, in their situation, a luxury indeed. They wanted, it is true, to add to their comfort, the provisions which they had brought from their retreat in the forest, but in the late attack, which dispersed their party, they were separated from the horses which had been laden with them. They huddled round the fire, and dried their cloaths. They discoursed with somewhat more cheerfulness than their conversation had of late displayed, and congratulated each other on their escape from the hands of Rhodolpho; 'till, exhausted with fatigue, sleep overtook them, and they sat slumbering over the dying embers, 'till they were rouzed by a noise which harrowed up the hearts of the females with terror, and appalled even the firm and manly breast of Anselmo.

A slow and solemn step, attended by the clashing of chains, seemed to gain upon their ears from a long passage opposite to that by which they had entered the kitchen.

Anselmo (for the lady Isabel and her companions, breathless and overcome with terror, shrunk behind their protector, and did not dare to cast their eyes towards the place whence the noise which alarmed them proceeded) beheld a light gleam at a distance on the walls of the passage, and soon after discerned the form of a man advancing slowly along it.

A deadly paleness overspread the countenance—the eyes were hollow, and sunk—the hair was clotted with blood—with which his garments were also stained, and the light which Anselmo had descried, proceeded from a taper which he held in his hand.

Anselmo's blood froze in his veins at this spectacle. In spite of all his fortitude his knees trembled, and a cold sweat bedewed his brow; nor could he arouse in his mind resolution enough to address the spectre before him, 'till he was awakened from this trance of terror by a singular phænomenon.

The form which has been described continued to advance, 'till it approached so near to Anselmo, that the light of the taper gleamed upon him; upon which he started suddenly, and prepared hastily to retreat.

Anselmo, roused by this circumstance, advanced to follow it; but the Princess Isabel and her Cousin shrieked aloud, and clung to him under the impulse of the most agonizing terror.

At their shrieks the phantom again turned towards them.

"Whatever thou art," cried Anselmo, "I conjure thee stay and relieve me from this horror."

"Anselmo!" exclaimed the spectre, in a hollow voice, but in a tone of perplexity and wonder.

The voice, hollow as it was, sounded like that of Rhinaldo. It recalled the wandering senses of Isabel. She looked in the face of the speaker, pale and disfigured as it was—it was the countenance of Rhinaldo too.

Isabel shrieked and fainted.

"Help, help my Cousin Isabel!" exclaimed Ellenor.

Rhinaldo, (for he was the spectre,) rushed forward to her assistance, while Anselmo remained motionless with wonder.

It was long before the beauteous Isabel could recover her scattered senses, and longer before she could be persuaded

that her Rhinaldo stood before her, impressed as she was
with the idea that it was the spirit of her departed lover
which she had seen.

Her doubts, however, at length subsided, and pity, at the
ghastly appearance of Rhinaldo, took place. She asked him,
with a mixture of affection, compassion, and horror, the
cause of his present appearance; and Rhinaldo, postponing
the gratification of his own curiosity, acquainted her with
his arrival at the forlorn mansion in which she saw him—the
death of the Count de St. Amand—and the discovery of
Count Tancred; after which he proceeded as follows:

"Rugiero had not long left us when we discovered that
the escape of that servant whom he had, without success,
attempted to detain, was as fatal a circumstance as his affectionate fears forboded that it would be.—This fellow went
immediately to a Castle of his lord's, which is at no great
distance from this, and alarmed the family with the story
of his death. Before we could settle any plan of escape, for
which my wound, though it was but slight, in some degree
still disqualified me, the house was assailed by the domestics of the Count. We barricaded it as well as we could, and
prevailed on the servants who remained with us to assist us
in our attempt to carry off the lady. We were preparing to
depart, when a postern door was forced, and our enemies
rushed in upon us. Count Tancred and I drew our swords, in
defence of the lady. I know no more—I was cut down—nor
did I recover my senses, 'till I found myself loaded with the
chains I now wear, and surrounded by a party of ruffians,
whom I had never before beheld. I was conducted into the
presence of Rhodolpho, who stood in the midst of a circle
of armed men. When he perceived who his prisoner was,
the hatred he had always borne towards me broke out in the
bitterest invectives, and he ordered me to be conveyed to the
dungeon from which I had rescued the Count Tancred.—
There my conductors left me. I heard the last door of my

prison close—in vain did I wait to hear it open again—hour after hour passed away—and the horrid silence of the dungeon continued uninterrupted. My remorseless foes had doomed me to all the horrors of a death by famine. I soon experienced many of its pangs. I awaked from my swoon to an intolerable thirst. Chained as I was, they had not taken the precaution to fix me to a particular spot, presuming, as I suppose, that I was well enough secured. I roved round my dungeon, raging under the agony of the thirst which consumed me, when I felt my foot touch something. Judge what was my transport, when I perceived this to be part of an earthen pitcher of water, which had been left there when Count Tancred was removed. But I will not dwell on circumstances which must afflict you. My wounds, though they had bled much, did not prove of much consequence. The horrors of my situation gave me strength and courage. I surveyed my dungeon, and by a feeble ray of light which entered at a narrow slip towards the roof, I descried a part of the wall bricked in the form of an arch. It immediately occurred to me that this had formerly been a door way, and that it might not be of the same substance as the rest of the wall. I sought again round my cavern for something with which I might remove a brick, and at least attempt to discover its thickness.—In searching near the stone to which my friend Tancred had been fastened, I most providentially discovered a dagger which I had used in attempting to free him from his chains, and had afterwards thrown carelessly by. With this I went to work.—The first brick I found much difficulty in removing—when that was done, my labour grew lighter in proportion; but many weary hours passed, before I had made an aperture big enough to admit my body. This, however, I at length accomplished, and found myself in a dungeon more horrid than that which I had quitted. It was lower than the other, and nothing more dismal, damp, and fætid, can be imagined. A few worn steps, just under the breach I had made, convinced me that that part of the wall had, as I had conjectured, been formerly a door-way——but I was soon too dreadfully convinced of it, by an object which, when I adverted to my own situation, curdled my blood with horror. By the faint light which gleamed through the aperture I had made, I discovered a rusty iron collar, chained to the wall—a hoop of iron, large enough to enclose the waist of a man, hung below it, close to the ground—and beneath it, amid a few rusted chains, and the tattered remnants of cloth which had escaped putrefaction, lay in a heap the skeleton of the wretch who had thus shrunk from his fetters. The horror with which I was struck at this spectacle, did not, however, prevent my exploring my new place of confinement. I could find no door. Alas! upon this unhappy victim, the only door to the dungeon had, probably, been walled up, as it was thought, for ever! In passing round this dungeon, I perceived the wind blow upon me from one corner, and, feeling the place, found that the walls were parted, either rifted by the bolt of heaven, or severed by the slow but sure hand of time. At this spot, then, I renewed my labour. I will not trouble you with a detail of it. After infinite toil, for, though more decayed, the wall at this place was much thicker than the former, I found my way, not many hours ago, into a narrow winding passage, thro' which I ascended into the house.—I proceeded, you may imagine, with extreme caution; nor did I discover all the horrors of my former situation, 'till I found that the whole of the premises were deserted, and I was left to undergo the fate of the miserable victim, whose remains I had so lately beheld. I just now discovered the remains of some salted provisions, of which I have had the prudence to eat but sparingly, and which, perhaps, may not be unwelcome to you. What is become of my friend Count Tancred and the lady, I cannot conjecture. She is, I suppose, carried off; and when I reflect on my own situation, I can scarcely entertain a hope that he is yet alive."

CHAP. IX.

WHEN Rhinaldo had finished his story, Anselmo related to him the distresses which had driven them to take shelter in a place which seemed so little calculated to produce so fortunate a meeting. Rhinaldo brought forth the little store of provisions which he had discovered. The fire was refreshed. Rhinaldo and Isabel blest that providence which had thus, when least expected, permitted them once more to behold each other, and to pour forth the delicate and chaste effusions of the sublimest of all passions, unchecked by harsh controul of pride, or the baneful mandates of a rigourous and unfeeling state policy.

Anselmo and his Ellenor were too much occupied with each other to interrupt them, nor would they, in spite of the remonstrances of Barbara, who had alone the discretion to reflect that their present situation was not wholly free from danger, have suffered a thought to intrude on the bliss of the moment, had not the step of some persons in the hall roused them from this state of oblivious happiness.

Anselmo, starting up, drew his sword, and Rhinaldo, whom his own exertions and those of his friend, tho' they could not wholly liberate, had freed from so much of chains, that they were no longer an incumbrance, seized the first weapon he could meet with, and they both moved towards the passage which led to the hall.

They perceived two men advancing towards them, one of whom bore a torch in his hand.

"Let us search," said he, who bore the torch, "through every corner of this seat of horrors. If he is alive I will find him."

Rhinaldo knew the voice of Tancred. "Count Tancred!

and living!" cried Rhinaldo; "thro' what miracle is it that I am again permitted to embrace my friend?"

"Rhinaldo!" exclaimed Tancred. "Then the object of my search is attained—blessed be heaven for the safety of my deliverer!"

"But how could you escape," resumed Rhinaldo, "the danger in which we were both involved?"

"Alas!" said Tancred, "I am indebted for my unhappy life to the loveliest—the best of women!—but no more of that—the thought is too much—Oh! let me but live to return the boon she gave!—to die for her!—but I rave——To make short of my story—When I last saw you, we were occupied in the defence of the Countess. While we were engaged with a party, too numerous for any but desperate men to contend with, another band seized the Countess, and bore her away. I left your side, my friend, and rushed to her assistance. I was struck down by a partizan—another arm was lifted for my destruction—the Countess caught hold of it—she put her purse into the hand of the soldier, and begged he would make his mistress his debtor, by saving my life. She promised the highest rewards. Interest, or, as I have reason to believe from his late conduct, humanity, determined this brave fellow. On the instant he bestrode me, fallen as I was, his comrades were quickly occupied in conveying away the Countess; and when he found himself free from observation, he raised me from the ground, and carried me to a private part of the Castle, whither, after the departure of Rhodolpho, he returned with his father, a woodman, of this forest, and conveyed me to his cottage. I had there so little recovered the effect of the blow I had received, that I scarcely knew what they did; but was soon re-established by the care that was taken of me. Behold my deliverer—he has resolved to share my fortune——"

As Count Tancred was proceeding, Rhinaldo was alarmed by the trampling of horses. They paused and listened—the noise increased—the voices of men were distinctly heard.

"We are surrounded," cried Anselmo. "Rhodolpho's party have traced us."

"There is then but one step to take," said Rhinaldo. "Follow me."

Isabel and her companions seemed now inured to terror. They suffered themselves to be led in silence. Rhinaldo conducted them up a back staircase, towards the room in which the Countess had been confined. They arrived at the little lumber room, which contained the battered armour. From this place Rhinaldo took the precaution to arm himself. He took down some of the swords, but they were wholly unserviceable. At last he chose a strong and heavy pole-axe, and shoving back the pannel, discovered to his friends the iron door. This door he opened, and bidding the forlorn party, which he conducted, enter the apartment, he replaced the pannel as carefully as possible, and joined his friends below.

They were convinced that the noise they had heard proceeded from some persons who had pursued them from the Castle of Rhodolpho, and who, probably, suspecting that if they should by chance have taken that road, they would retire to the old mansion for shelter, or, perhaps, attracted by the light of the fire they had kindled, or of the taper which Rhinaldo had procured, were induced to search for them there.

They formed many conjectures as to the number of their enemies; at the supposed magnitude of which they were not so much alarmed, as at the idea that Rhodolpho might be among them, who had, most probably, been acquainted by his father with the secret of the pannel—a secret, as yet, perhaps, undivulged to any other person.

Their fears, however, as to the presence of Rhodolpho, proved on this occasion unfounded. He was on the succeeding day to join Astolpho with his company of men at arms, and had only detached on this pursuit a pretty numerous train of domestics, well armed, and headed by two of his most trusty adherents.

While they stood wrapt in these conjectures, and in a mournful silence the result of them, they were aroused by the sound of many steps ascending the stairs, which led to the little lumber-room. They listened in a state of breathless expectation and terror.—They had not yet closed to the iron door; nor indeed could its strength avail them, as all the fastnings were on the outer side.

They heard a person walk slowly round the lumber room. What were their sensations when he exclaimed, "We can go no farther this way—let us return."

This was assented to by a companion who was with him, and they heard, with a rapture scarcely to be described, their returning footsteps on the staircase which they had just ascended.

Rhinaldo and his companions continued in their place of concealment for half an hour, before they judged it prudent to make any attempt towards discovering whether their pursuers had retired; for, in their secluded situation, they could hear nothing.

Rhinaldo then slowly began to open the pannel, when an object presented itself, which induced him to close it again with a haste which struck a sudden terror to the hearts of his companions.

This object was the face of a man. This person, who bore a light in his hand, was ascending the staircase when Rhinaldo perceived him, who encouraged a faint hope, that, from the distance he was at, the taper he bore could not cast any strong reflection on the walls of the room.

This hope, however, soon died away. They heard a clattering noise against the pannel itself, and immediately prepared themselves to receive this intruder in such a manner as to prevent, if possible, any discovery through his means.

In a short time afterwards the noise ceased, and they heard the footsteps of this person descending the staircase, as they immediately conjectured, to procure assistance.

They now gave themselves up for lost, and an hour passed before Rhinaldo dared again attempt to open the pannel. He proceeded cautiously; but his effort was accompanied by a noise he could not account for; and a heavy object fell inwards against his legs. This he soon discovered to be a cuirass, which indeed the person who had caused them so much alarm had placed there.

This person had returned to this ancient armoury, to try if he could accommodate himself with some pieces of more value than his own—but probably retired disappointed in his aim.

Rhinaldo now recovered from this new alarm, and proceeded cautiously towards the head of the great staircase. When he arrived there, he heard the murmur of voices at the door of the hall, and found that their pursuers, tired of their vain search, were about to mount their horses and retire. He waited 'till he heard them pass over the drawbridge, and then returning to his friends, acquainted them with this event.

Upon intelligence so welcome, they quitted their place of concealment, and after waiting 'till they judged that their pursuers had proceeded far enough to insure them from the danger of a discovery, they sallied from these crazy walls, and left this forlorn mansion for ever!

They had no sooner gained the forest, than Isabel, throwing her arms round her Cousin, and faithful attendant, mingled her tears with theirs; and Rhinaldo and Anselmo, pressing Isabel and Ellenor gently to their breasts, joined with them in pouring forth their thanks to heaven for their signal deliverance; while Count Tancred contemplated, in deep and silent sorrow, the mysterious fate which involved that adored object, for whom alone he thought the life he had so lately retrieved worth preserving.

END OF THE FIRST VOLUME.

COUNT RODERIC's CASTLE.

CHAP. X.

THOUGH Rhinaldo, the Lady Isabel, and their friends, were delivered from their late peril, it was still a matter of serious deliberation in what manner they should now proceed. To remain where they were 'till the day should dawn, would render them liable to all the dangers that might result from a discovery. It was resolved, therefore, dark as the night was, to proceed, and they travelled onward, 'till the day broke upon them, in a small opening of the forest.

A stream, which broke from the summit of a lofty cliff, that bounded them on one side, and ran murmuring along the foot of it, tempted them to halt here for a short time, and take that repose, of which they were so much in need. After drinking of this stream, and resting themselves, they pursued their journey.

Though the dread of being overtaken had supported them thro' more than common exertions, yet nature began, at length, to be exhausted—and Isabel, dissolving into tears, declared that she must die where she was, for she could proceed no farther; saying this, she sunk into Rhinaldo's arms, who laid her gently on the turf, and, supporting her head on his breast, hung over her in all the agony of the most piercing despair.

Anselmo, Ellenor, and Barbara, (the two latter of whom felt a degree of faintness and lassitude almost equal to that of the fainting Isabel,) knew not what to do. At length Anselmo perceiving that the cliff, from which the stream took its course, still appeared through the tops of the trees on his right hand, proposed to Count Tancred, if possible, to climb it, that from its summit they might explore the country around, under the precarious hope that some relief might possibly be at hand. Impressed with this idea, they made their way towards it, and had scarcely gained the margin of the rivulet, when, to their infinite surprise and joy, they saw the eminence terminate at some distance from them, by an easy descent, interspersed with clumps of trees, leaving the rivulet to wind through a beautiful valley, which divided the forest as far as the eye could reach.

At the bottom of this descent, and close on the banks of the rivulet, they discovered a cottage, and hastened towards it, to endeavour to procure relief.

They had scarcely gained the wooden bridge, by which it communicated with the valley, when a man advanced from the cottage door to meet them. What was the surprise of Anselmo, when he perceived this man to be Rugiero.

After expressing his astonishment at a meeting so unexpected, he communicated to Rugiero the situation in which he had left his companions, and they returned to the spot where Isabel had sunk under her fatigue. They found her still supported by Rhinaldo, and her Cousin and attendant sitting by her, in a dreary silence. Intelligence of the unexpected relief which was at hand gave some animation to their drooping spirits.

Isabel arose, with the assistance of Rhinaldo, and leaning on his arm, and upheld by Count Tancred on the other side, she followed Anselmo, who supported the feeble steps of his weary Ellenor, while Rugiero served them as a guide, and Barbara leaning on the attendant of Count Tancred, followed her lady.

The owner of the dwelling received them with an honest

though rustic hospitality. He desired his wife, who was nothing backward in her civilities, to attend to the lady, for as yet he discovered but one, while he prepared a homely meal for the rest, whom he perceived to stand in great need of refreshment.

Isabel and Ellenor were conducted by the old woman, after she had been informed of the secret of their sex, to a comfortable bed, on which they threw themselves without undressing; and Barbara, at their desire, placing herself by their side, they soon fell into a sound and refreshing sleep.

During this period, Rugiero visited Rhinaldo's wounds. They had been originally slight, and a good constitution had already so far contributed to their cure, that this skilful domestic found his labours limited to the freeing his master from the traces of the blood which had originally issued from them. Having therefore dressed him as well as the bareness of his toilet would permit, and persuaded him to take, in an easy chair, that repose of which he stood so much in need, he related to Count Anselmo those circumstances, which had happened to him since they had lost him in the forest. He told him of the accident which had happened to his horse, which he had reason to believe never rose from the spot where he fell.

"I waited," continued Rugiero, "under the tree, to which I had crept for shelter, 'till the storm had in some measure abated, when I returned to try if I could raise my horse. After several efforts I found it impracticable, and was finally obliged to give over the attempt, on hearing the trampling of a body of horsemen on the road. As it appeared to me probable that these were of Count Rhodolpho's party, I turned immediately out of the path, and making across the forest, which at that place is tolerably open, I had the good luck, before I had proceeded far, to arrive at the banks of this rivulet, and, finding no bridge across it, pursued my path along its margin, 'till I discovered this cottage.

"The old pair, who inhabit it, are vassals to Count Rhodolpho, but having hoarded some money in the service of the father of the late Count de St. Amand, are in easy circumstances.—This I learned from themselves on my arrival. They appear to be honest people, yet I cannot conceal from your lordship my apprehensions that we are by no means in safety here. It cannot be far from the road which I quitted, when I heard the trampling of horses, and by which you found your way from one Castle to the other. If Count Rhodolpho should disperse his party through the forest in search of us, some of them will, in all probability, find their way to this cottage."

After a few hours passed in sleep, the Lady Isabel arose, much refreshed, and awakening her Cousin and attendant, they joined Rhinaldo and his friends.

A consultation again took place.—Anselmo communicated to his friends the fears of Rugiero, and it was agreed, after some deliberation, that they should seek the Castle of Count Roderic, Rhinaldo's father, where they deemed themselves sure of protection.

Though they were not acquainted with the direct road to it, they knew in what part of the country it lay; and Rugiero hesitated not to declare, that he thought he could undertake to conduct them towards it. Having then gratified their kind hosts, and provided themselves with some refreshments for their journey, they departed, and crossing into a thicker part of the forest, to avoid being discovered, they turned their steps towards that part of the country in which Rugiero conjectured the Count Roderic's Castle lay.

After a march of some hours, they stopped to refresh themselves, and setting forward again, pursued their journey 'till the shades of evening began again to overtake them.

Though they had travelled far, there was yet no appearance of the Castle; and from the answers of Rugiero, to the incessant questions which the fears of Lady Isabel suggested, it was perceived that he was at least more diffident of his knowledge than he had been in the morning.

This discovery had an effect on the spirits of the whole party. The necessity of subjecting their fair companions, for another night, to the inclemency of the skies, gave a double portion of anguish to the breasts of Anselmo and Rhinaldo, and they moved onward in a mournful silence, which every one seemed too much occupied by his own thoughts to interrupt.

As they were thus slowly travelling onward, they arrived at a rising ground, on which was erected a stone cross.— This mark Rugiero no sooner perceived, than he suddenly exclaimed that he knew the spot.

"To the right," said he, "is an hermitage belonging to the Convent of St. Julian; and to the left, within the distance of half a mile, the road which leads to Count Roderic's Castle, which cannot be more than six miles from us."

Anselmo proposed that they should turn towards the hermitage, where the Lady Isabel and her Cousin, who seemed worn out with fatigue, might rest 'till the morning; but these ladies appeared to have collected fresh spirits from the information of Rugiero, and anxious to arrive at a place of safety, declared that they were very well enabled to reach the Castle, urging Rhinaldo to proceed with so much eagerness, that the plan was, as it turned out, most unluckily adopted.

They soon reached the road, but had not travelled far along it, when, as they turned the corner of a wood, which projected towards the road, they were overtaken by a troop of cavalry, who had no sooner discovered, than they gallopped immediately towards them.

At the head of this troop they quickly discovered Rhodolpho, who immediately ordered them to be surrounded and disarmed.

The horsemen, who consisted of Rhodolpho's company

of men at arms, attended by their valets, immediately pressed upon them.

Rhinaldo, prepared to defend the Princess and her Cousin to the last extremity, drew up his little band, with their backs to the wood, and seeing Rhodolpho press onwards with the rest, sprung forward, and aimed a blow at him with his pole-axe, which, as he stooped to avoid it, alighted on his shoulder, and brought him to the ground.

It pierced his corslet, and, had he not been completely armed, as were all his troop, would, though it had not proved fatal, have probably disabled him for ever.

This accident occupied part of his troop, who surrounded him. As soon as he recovered himself, he gave orders that the women, whose habits he described, should be seized, while the men were engaged, and carried off.

The command was speedily executed by the valets, who, bring unarmed, could the more readily dismount.—While Rhinaldo and his friends were pressed by the horsemen, these fellows seized on the Princess and her companions, and in spite of their efforts, their tears and supplications, bore them away.

This was not done without opposition from their little party, who, upon hearing the shrieks of the women, made a daring effort to join them; but pressed on all sides by the horsemen, another body of whom formed up to cover the retreat of those who bore off the Princess, they were finally compelled to retire, and seek shelter in the wood, which they did without difficulty, for the horsemen, who were completely and heavily armed, having no room to charge them, found themselves rather incumbered than assisted by their lances, and they could not dismount to assail them in the wood; they therefore, when they found their enemies secured from any farther attack, and the prize they had contended for attained, retired after their companions.

It would be difficult to paint the despair which seized

on Rhinaldo and Anselmo at this fatal event. A thousand schemes, suggested by grief and indignation, presented themselves to them. They purposed following the ravishers, many and formidable as they were; but they could never hope to overtake them.

It was at last resolved that they should pursue their way to the Castle, when their attention was called towards Count Tancred, who was sitting at the foot of a tree. He had received a wound, from the thrust of a lance, in his arm, and it bled so profusely, that there was little hope of his being able to walk so far as to the Castle that evening; and Rugiero, who bound up his wound, proposed that they should seek shelter for the night at the hermitage he had mentioned, which was at no great distance, and proceed in the morning towards the Castle. This advice was, in their present situation, too salutary to be neglected, and they returned to the stone cross, which they had so lately left, whence Rugiero conducted them to the hermitage.

CHAP. XI.

THE venerable inhabitant of the place had not yet lighted his lamp, but sat at the door of his cavern, wrapt in meditation. He advanced to meet them with a benevolent smile, and offered them the shelter of his lowly roof, in terms which a long acquaintance, with the more polished society among mankind, could alone communicate; and he no sooner perceived the situation of Count Tancred, than he produced some medicinal stores, for which he was much famed among the neighbouring poor, and inspecting the wound, applied to it a dressing, from the experienced virtues of which he promised himself a speedy success. He then "spread his vegetable store" before his guests; nor was this all——the gratitude of his rustic neighbours had supplied him with more substantial food, of which he sometimes, though sparingly, partook.

He could not but perceive the gloom and despondency which hung over some of his guests, and which all their efforts to gratify him by a cheerful acceptance of his favours, could not dispel; but his skill in mankind had taught him, that where grief admits of alleviation, by being participated, it will obtrude itself; and that where it seeks concealment, it is generally too poignant to be relieved by communication.

Rhinaldo, however, who knew not of any motive he had to conceal himself so near to his father's Castle, and who, had any such motive occurred, would have disdained a concealment with any one who belonged to the convent of St. Julian, made himself readily known to the hermit, and introduced his friends Anselmo and Tancred.

The venerable hermit received this communication with politeness, but a visible reserve hung over him during the rest of the repast, which Rugiero, the most unconcerned of the guests, except Count Tancred's deliverer, was the first to notice.

It perplexed this faithful servant, and he watched an opportunity to communicate his observation to his master.—This, however, he waited in vain to obtain.

The hermit, as soon as their frugal repast was finished, begged that Rhinaldo would indulge him, by accompanying him round his little domains, which it had been for many years his daily task to beautify; and his other guests, perceiving that they were not included in this invitation, suffered Rhinaldo, who readily accepted of this offer, to accompany him alone.

The moon had now arisen, and, after some general observations on the beauty of the place, which, at such a season, would have had a thousand charms for any bosom less torn with conflicting passions than that of Rhinaldo, the hermit addressed him as follows:

"Count Rhinaldo, I am doomed to communicate to you intelligence, of which I find by your conversation you are yet ignorant, and which must severely afflict you."

"Proceed," said Rhinaldo, firmly—"after what I have suffered today, all other sorrows must be light."

"Count Roderic's Castle," continued the hermit, "is in the hands of the king."

"Has my father then," said Rhinaldo, in a tone of grief, "sided with the usurper? Alas! why was not I permitted to communicate to him that secret, the concealment of which has produced so much mischief; for had he known that his lawful sovereign—"

"Alas!" said the hermit, "your father is himself a prisoner, if——if——he lives."

"If he lives!" said Rhinaldo, starting back, and a visible paleness overspread his countenance.

"This king," said the hermit, "surprized him—no sooner had the plot, in which you embarked, failed, than Astolpho set out hastily for the frontiers. He arrived here before any intelligence could be received, and desired admission to the Castle, as your father's guest, for a few days. Your father, unconscious that he could have any fresh cause of displeasure, and indeed unable, on so sudden an occasion, to prevent his admission, was compelled to receive him; and he was very speedily followed by a force which would have proved formidable, had his intention been divulged. Thus has he contrived to sit down before his enemies, occupying a very formidable post. Our friends, however, yet possess the mount of St. Julian, where they are very strong."

"And has no intelligence of the fate of my father yet reached you?"

"None, but the melancholy and uncertain rumour which I have already disclosed to you."

Rhinaldo seemed wrapt, for a moment, in gloomy reflections. He started, after a pause, from his reverie.—"And father Anthony?" said Rhinaldo, in a hesitating voice.

"My son, I commend thy caution," said the hermit; "but father Anthony is now acknowledged for that which he is. Yes," continued the venerable anchorite, his eyes gleaming with the fire of youth as he spoke, "our lawful lord and sovereign, Emanuel, commands the forces on Mount St. Julian, and may success attend his arms! His situation indeed, at present, is not without danger; but if the diversion on the western frontiers, which is already formidable, should draw off any strong detachment of Astolpho's forces, what may we not expect?"

"Thou speakest with a fire that would shame the tardiness of younger men, father," said Rhinaldo.

"Would I could join my brethren of the Mount in arms!" replied the hermit. "But even here I may not prove wholly useless."

Rhinaldo now returned to join his friends, and the hermit spread before them some mats, the work of his own hands, composed of grass and rushes; but the softest down could not have allured Rhinaldo to slumber. He revolved in his mind the situation of his father; and the loss of Isabel, which had so deeply afflicted him, seemed to lose some of the bitterness with which it had overwhelmed him.

He judged that his own conduct, which he now censured as hasty and rash, had involved that honoured parent in disgrace and ruin—perhaps had given him up a prey to the knife of the secret assassin. He could not for a moment endure the pang of a thought so pregnant with horror. He resolved at all events to proceed to the Castle, and learn the fate of his father, that, if he still lived, he might learn his destiny, and participate his misfortunes; and, if dead, might revenge his death, or devote himself a sacrifice to the fatal consequences of his rash and mysterious enterprise.

Anselmo, whose loss would not permit him to enjoy a larger portion of repose than fell to the lot of Rhinaldo, left his couch with the first dawn of day, and perceived his friend already risen, and tracing, with pensive step, the beautiful, yet gloomy recesses, with which the neighbourhood of the hermitage abounded.

Here Rhinaldo related to him the intelligence which he had received from the hermit, and concluded with his fixed determination to disguise himself, and at all events, if possible, gain access to the Castle.

The venerable father now joined them, and having in vain endeavoured to point out to Rhinaldo the rashness of his undertaking, was compelled to acquiesce in his determination, and offered to assist in preparing him for the perpetration of his design.

Anselmo, when he heard that the rallying point of the party which had been so unsuccessful in the enterprise, of which he had been the leader, was so near the spot where he now was, resolved to join the faithful adherents of Emanuel at the convent of St. Julian; and received intelligence from the hermit of a pass by which he might gain the out-posts, avoiding at the same time the troops of Astolpho, and a secret word, which would procure him ready admission to their leaders.

Rhinaldo, in pursuance of his design, cut his hair close to his head; and having otherwise, by the assistance and advice of his friends, so disguised his person, that there was little dread of his being discovered, changed his dress for that of the man who had attended Count Tancred, and, having taken a friendly leave of that nobleman, whose wound became so much inflamed, as to threaten him with some confinement in the hermitage, he departed, accompanied by Count Anselmo and his faithful Rugiero.

When they had proceeded about three miles on their journey, Count Anselmo, accompanied by Rugiero, whom his lord, in spite of all his intreaties, refused to admit to a share in the adventure he was about to undertake, lest his presence should lead to a discovery, quitted Rhinaldo to pursue the road which the hermit had pointed out to him.

Deep in meditation on his intended scheme, and revolving in his mind plan after plan, now adopting and now rejecting them, as they offered themselves for his consideration, Rhinaldo came within sight of his father's Castle, before any settled system of operation had suggested itself to him.

While he was thus musing, his eyes fixed with a mournful gaze on the well-known turrets, which recalled to his memory many of the cheerful and innocent hours of childhood, he came suddenly upon a guard of Astolpho's soldiers, who were posted on one of the avenues to the Castle.

The centinel who was on duty asked him who he was? and where he was going? As he was hesitating what answer he should give, he perceived the corporal, who was commanding officer of this party, miserably thrumming upon a harp.

He answered, "that he was a poor harper, who had been robbed in the forest of that which was the only means of his subsistence—his harp."

This was a lure, from which he hoped to derive some advantage, for he was well skilled in this instrument, which had formed great part of his amusement during his youthful days. Nor was he deceived in his expectations. The corporal arose upon hearing this, and, giving him the instrument, desired him to play. He had no sooner touched it, than the whole guard forgot their duty. They received him as if he had been an old acquaintance, and the corporal placing him on the seat which he had just occupied, they sat in a circle round him, listening to the strains which flowed from his instrument in silent rapture.

To this officer he particularly attached himself, and so won upon him, by imparting to him a few instructions concerning the instrument he so much admired, that when he was relieved, he swore he would not part with so valuable a friend, but conducted him to the guardhouse of the Castle.

He was soon familiarized among the soldiers, and frequently urged to enlist among them, but telling his friend, the corporal, frankly, that he did not like the situation, and wished to be placed in service, that officer soon introduced him to one of the servants of the house, who was like himself fond of music; and by the good offices of this patron, Rhinaldo became soon enrolled among the liveried attendants on Astolpho.

CHAP. XII.

THUS introduced to his paternal mansion, he mingled unnoticed with the servile herd, among whom he was enrolled, and traced, in this obscure situation, those stately apartments, which had rung with gratulatory acclamations at his birth, and where his youth had been fostered with the most anxious care.

The splendid armour which adorned the hall, had proved the hardy deeds of a long line of warlike ancestors; and the banners which waved over them, were badges of their illustrious descent.

On the morning succeeding the day of his admission to the Castle, as he was employed, with others, in preparing a repast, Astolpho, attended by the chief officers who had accompanied him on this expedition, entered the hall. He was leaning on one of his train in close and familiar converse. How was the indignation of Rhinaldo aroused, when he found this favourite to be his cruel enemy Rhodolpho!

A thousand ideas obtruded themselves at once on his mind. Conflicting passions assailed his bosom, over which rage and revenge predominated, and he was on the point of rushing, unarmed and helpless as he was, upon his rancarous enemy, and attempting to sacrifice him, even at the side of Astolpho, a victim to his own wrongs, and the tears of his adored Isabel. But the idea of this lovely maiden presented itself to his imagination, at a fortunate period, to check the wild frenzy which had seized him.

Rhodolpho was in the Castle. Was it not probable that Isabel was there too? The hope, faint as it at first appeared, that she might, even now, be under the same roof with him—that, unknown as he was, some favourable opportunity of serving her might occur to him, soothed his transports, and he retired, as soon as the duties of his office would permit him, to meditate, in solitude, on a subject, which so amply engrossed his contemplation. But he had soon, alas! a deeper subject for meditation; for

> "Meditation, even to madness."

It was no longer a subject of doubt or concealment in the Castle, that Roderic the Hardy, the lord of the domain, the father of Rhinaldo! had been murdered, within half a league of the Castle, and the finger of suspicion pointed at Astolpho.

Indeed, when the circumstances attending this transaction were considered, little doubt could be entertained on the subject.

Roderic had not been seen since he had welcomed the king to the Castle.

A very short time had sufficed to acquaint him with Astolpho's design, and at day-break on the ensuing morning, (for it was evening when Astolpho arrived,) he had departed, completely armed, with a few trusty attendants. It was thought that Astolpho was aware of this departure, and winked at it, though Count Roderic could have but one design in it, which was to join his friends in the west, for, within half a league of the Castle, he was set upon by a party, and killed with the shot of an arquebuss, pointed directly at his breast, so close that his corslet was unable to resist the balls.

Not one of his attendants escaped; but the transaction

was witnessed by some who knew his armour. They sought afterwards for the body, but that, as well as those of his attendants, was carried off, and probably for reasons known to Astolpho, if he were really the author of this murder, buried in some secret place.

The reflections of Rhinaldo upon this horrid catastrophe, were the most bitter that unbounded grief and unavailing remorse could furnish. He looked upon himself as the murderer of his father. A settled gloom overspread his mind, and nothing but the hope of revenge could have instigated him to perform the task he had undertaken, or have procrastinated, for a moment, a discovery which must have proved fatal to him.

From these more than melancholy reflections, he was roused by intelligence which diverted his affections into a different channel. He learned that the Princess was actually, as he suspected, in the Castle; but nobody whom he could converse with had yet seen her. It was also reported that Rhodolpho was soon to be married to her.

Rhinaldo, acquainted as he was with the Castle from the days of his earliest youth, knew that, if she was actually there, she could not be long concealed from him, and resolved to watch the motions of Rhodolpho with a scrutinizing eye.

In the mean time hostilities were vigourously carried on between the two parties.

Astolpho had a very strong force with him at the Castle, with which he continued to make vigourous assaults against the Priory; but, besides that, that post was almost impregnable—it was defended by the most brave and experienced knights——for such had been the fathers of St. Julian, before they devoted their days to the duties of religion.

The wound which had detained Count Tancred at the hermitage, proved more obstinate than he had expected; nor did the state of his mind in any way contribute to the forwarding its cure; but he found, in the conversation of the venerable hermit, much alleviation to his sorrows.

This holy father, who had long trod, in a distinguished character, the busy stage of the world, had not viewed mankind without observation. His mind was, therefore, amply stored with true wisdom, that which is born of sound reflection upon long experience, and the sublime truths of religion had softened his heart to the frailties and infirmities of his fellow-creatures, while they spread over his breast that delicious calm which they alone are capable of bestowing.

Count Tancred, who, in communicating his griefs to such a man, found the only alleviation to his sorrows of which they were capable, soon entrusted to him the secret of that melancholy, to which it was too apparent his heart was a prey.

CHAP. XIII.

YOU will not, my venerable father," said the Count, "long wonder at the weight which oppresses my soul, and which, in spite of all efforts to throw it off, still baffles my endeavours, when I relate to you my unhappy story.

"You are not ignorant, that our monarch Astolpho, sur-named the Proud, had a sister many years younger than himself, whom, when upon the death of the great and good Emanuel, he mounted the throne of Lombardy, he drew from the retirement in which she had been 'till that period immured.

"The Princess Aspasia was at this time of such tender years, that it was not judged proper to detain her long at court. The Castle of Montalban, than which none can be more delightfully situated, was fitted up in a most princely manner for her residence; and her household was established under the government and direction of a lady, her relation.

"Of this establishment I had, what I then esteemed, the good fortune to make one. In an age, little advanced beyond that of infancy, I was appointed one of the pages to the Princess.

"Let me pass over, my venerable father, those hours, in which the seeds of a passion, which I shall carry with me to the grave, began to unfold themselves.

"Those delicious moments, which were incessantly marked by sensations as sweet as undefined, are awakened to the memory, only to embitter, by obtruding themselves into a comparison with others which have been as strongly tinctured with complicated misery.

"What was at first duty, soon grew to be something more—and, surely, no hours can be more sweetly passed than those in which his duties of station are stimulated by affection, and have the reward of not passing unnoticed by their object.

"The Princess soon distinguished me—I adored her—we grew up together, and our passion strengthened with our years.

"Let me hasten to the conclusion of a tale, which too much oppresses me.

"In the time of the late wars, Astolpho scarcely during three years resided for three months in the capital. The Princess, though of an age to grace the most distinguished circles, by her understanding as well as her beauty, seemed to be forgotten, and remained, without a murmur on her part, at the Castle of Montalban.

"Happy period! Period! made up of the most delicious moments! To see her daily—to attend her as the sweetest, the most grateful of duties urged me, was all my full satisfied heart had learned to wish! Alas! it was too soon to end. I became of an age, when it was deemed improper that I should remain idle at home.

"I was appointed to a command; and, with as much alacrity as a man can possess, who leaves behind him all to which his heart has learned to cleave, I joined the army. I was then stationed with the same brigade as Rhinaldo, and it was our fortune to see some severe service together. I returned about the time when Astolpho ordered the Princess to court. She there became the theme of ceaseless admiration.

"Astolpho himself seemed to adore her, when suddenly, contrary to all expectations, in spite of her detestation towards the object—of her prayers and supplications—of the groans she uttered—and the tears she shed at his feet— he sacrificed her to his stern and brutal favourite, the Count St. Amand.

"Proud, vindictive, and remorseless, this man seemed little softened by the beauties which inflamed him; but bore his wretched victim to a dreary Castle on the north of this forest, where, in solitude, she was left to shed unavailing tears over the miserable fate to which the unaccountable partiality of a brother, who, she had reason to believe, loved her, had consigned her a helpless prey.

"What, alas! was my situation during this dreadful period! My despair was not to be concealed. It became so marked, that the cause of it began to be whispered at court. My frantic love at length, no longer to be restrained, burst forth in an act, which involved the object of it, as well as myself, in the most wretched calamity.

"I determined to obtain an interview, a last one, with the Princess, and then seek in a foreign war that death, which the peaceful state of my own country then denied to my wishes.

"Unhappy resolution! I bribed her servants, and gained admittance to her presence. She was in her chamber, which she seldom quitted. I found her employed in adding some ornaments to a mantle of state which she had formerly embroidered and destined for me, upon Astolpho's promising, at her intercession, to appoint me, young as I was, to the office of Knight Marshal, which is, as you well know, a post of great honour, and to which my birth alone, though it is not inconsiderable, could scarcely, at so early a period, have entitled me.

"She was weeping—weeping, as she confessed, in an agony of sorrow, as soon as her resentment at the rash action of which I had been guilty had subsided, over the memory of the unfortunate Tancred.

"Let me hurry over this delicious though fatal interview. I told her my resolve—we were both in tears—I was kneeling at her feet, bidding her adieu, and had my lips pressed to her lovely hand, which was wet with my tears, and on which I imprinted a last kiss, and was rising to tear myself away for ever—when the Count, whether apprised by the servants I had corrupted, or incited by the rumours which prevailed at Court, and the settled sorrow and disgust which the Princess could not conceal at the sacrifice she had been compelled to make, burst into the room, attended by a numerous train of servants.

"I was about to draw my sword, when I was seized and disarmed.

"The brutality of the Count's nature now raged uncontrouled. He drew a poignard, as if about to murder his wife in my presence; but a thought of a deeper revenge seemed to check this purpose. He smiled grimly on her, and, sheathing the dagger, ordered me to be carried to a place of security.

"We were both of us, the next morning, before the day broke, conveyed secretly to a ruinous mansion, which he possesses, situate on the verge of the forest, attended by himself and two servants, in whom he chiefly confided.

"The miseries which the unhappy Aspasia endured, from the savage and unbridled cruelty of this monster, during a month's confinement in that desolate mansion, she alone can tell.

"I was the tenant of a loathsome dungeon, from which the hand of Providence, and the courage and conduct of my friend Rhinaldo, relieved me. In what manner you have heard from himself. You have also heard how the Princess was again torn from us. But let me perish ignobly, if I do not discover the miscreant Rhodolpho, the base son of this inhuman father, if the earth does not conceal him. I will tear him from the side of his master, in whose favour he hath supplanted his father, rather than forego the revenge for which my soul thirsts."

CHAP. XIV.

THE hermit strove to calm the violent agitation, which he perceived the relation of Count Tancred had raised in his bosom, and, having soothed him to some degree of tranquillity, addressed him as follows:

"Alas! my son, let not your rage induce you to attempt impossibilities; but await 'till circumstances shall bereave your enemies of that power, of which they are now, too fatally, possessed.

"Rhodolpho is as firmly fixed as his father was in the favour of Astolpho; and were another sister to be sacrificed, dear to that monarch as was Albina, she would instantaneously become the sacrifice of this connexion.

"Of the cause of this I have learned from Rhinaldo that you are ignorant—but I do not fear to trust you with it. Listen then to the story I shall relate:——

"It is now about fifteen years since Lombardy sustained a loss, which it has never yet recovered, in our great and good Emanuel, when this half-brother Astolpho ascended the throne. It was generally thought that Emanuel had perished in a hunting party, in which he was separated from his attendants, and in spite of all those inquiries which the anxiety of a whole people promoted, he was never, for the space of above fourteen years, heard of.

"This supposition was rendered the more probable, as the part of the forest in which he was missed abounded with wolves of the largest and most ravenous kind.

"His dauntless courage—the wisdom which was displayed in every act of his government—the mildness and urbanity of his address and manners, rendered the loss of such a king universally regretted. Nor was it without symptoms of gloom and dissatisfaction that Astolpho's title to the crown was confessed; and the daughter of Emanuel, though then in the age of absolute infancy, did not want partizans, who suggested in very loud terms her right to the throne.

"The party of Astolpho, however, who was indisputably brave and skilful in the field, and who possessed some of those virtues which allure popularity, soon silenced these murmurers, and he was proclaimed king.

"Fourteen years had elapsed since this event took place, when a stranger, poorly clad, but of a dignified and majestic mien, arrived towards the fall of night at the Priory of St. Julian, and demanded of the superiour admission into the brotherhood, pledging himself to make good his claim on the succeeding day.

"The necessary qualification for a brother of our order is, that the candidate be a knight, who has for fifteen years served his country bravely, faithfully, and without reproach.

"The stranger was presented with some refreshment after his journey, and conveyed to a cell, where he was left to repose himself 'till the morning, when he was desired to attend the superior of the order.

"When the stranger was admitted into the presence of the superior, he asked him "if he knew him?"

"The old man, who had lived for above thirty years in that retirement, had lost all traces of his countenance.

"My father!" exclaimed the stranger, "if your pupil Emanuel, who followed your steps so inadequately at the battle of the Bucklers[1], should be still living, might he hope protection from the brothers of St. Julian?"

"The good old man arose from his seat at these words, and approached the stranger, for his eyes had begun already to grow dim with age. He surveyed him for a short time, and then falling at his feet, and embracing his knees,—"I have lived long enough!" exclaimed the venerable soldier; "am I permitted once more to behold my sovereign!—one who has so long been the pride of my heart!—one whose death my age has so long lamented."

"Emanuel (for he was the stranger) raising the old man, folded him in his arms, and asked him whether he might confide a secret, on which his life depended, to the rest of the fathers!

"Of this indeed he little doubted. He knew them all—for they had all been the companions of his youth, as renowned for their courage as their conduct, and he easily gave credit to the venerable prior, when he took upon himself to answer for their fidelity.

"They were immediately summoned, and Emanuel discovered himself to them, and related the circumstances of the mysterious fate which enveloped him, nearly as follows:——

CHAP. XV.

ON the day which first beheld me torn from my kingdom, and doomed for fourteen years to a state of dreary and melancholy confinement, I was pursuing the chace with my wonted eagerness, and found myself, through the swiftness of my horse, separated from all my companions and

1 So called from a corps of infantry called Buckler Men, who fought with sword and target, and whose gallant stand under the shelter of their bucklers, which were exceedingly large, saved the right wing of the army; commanded by the father of Emanuel in person, and turned the fortune of the day.

attendants, except my brother Astolpho, and his friend the Count St. Amand, who had changed their horses, and were thus enabled to keep up with me.

"After riding for some considerable time, and finding ourselves involved in the most intricate part of the forest, notwithstanding the skill of the Count de St. Amand, who undertook to guide us, it was proposed by that nobleman that we should seek refreshment at a mansion of his, which he said he was sure could be at no great distance from the part of the forest in which we then were.

"It proved, as he had conjectured, that we were near to this spot, and a short time conducted us to it. It was an old building, spacious, and formerly, no doubt, magnificent.

"The Count apologized for the reception we were about to meet with, in a house where he maintained but few servants, and where he seldom resided. It did not, therefore, appear singular to me to be welcomed only by a single domestic who received orders to attend to our horses, and procure us some refreshment; while we were conducted by the Count himself to a spacious apartment. There a collation was soon spread, and we ate like men who had rode hard all the morning.

"After dinner the Count proposed to shew us the house, in the construction of which, old as it was, he said there were some things deserving attention.

"After viewing many apartments, we were conducted up a staircase into a small room, in which were deposited various pieces of armour; from this room, slipping aside a pannel of the wainscot which concealed a door strongly fortified with iron, the Count led us into an apartment tolerably spacious, but very gloomy, furnished with a bed, and other conveniencies of a stately structure, but of very antique fashion.

"In this apartment I was much surprised to find a man of a stern ferocious countenance, and a robust make, whom, though I had not much noticed him before, I soon perceived to be the servant who had attended at our entrance. He was armed with a cuirass, had a sword by his side, a dagger in his girdle, and held a partizan in his hand.

"I observed, with some surprise, that he did not move his hat, which he had on, at our approach; and a little alarmed at this circumstance, as well as his general appearance, from my own defenceless state, (for I had set out in the morning armed only with a cutlass for the chace, which I had unbuckled and thrown aside, during our repast, after the example of my brother and the Count,) I turned round to look for Astolpho, and perceived that he had not entered the room with us.

"I had no time to waste in conjectures on this circumstance. The Count shut the door behind him, and, advancing towards the man, seized the partizan which he held in his hand, and pointing it to my breast, swore vehemently that if I ventured to stir, I should die.

"He then desired the fellow to do his duty, who, reaching down a pair of manacles, which were hung to the wall, came forward to bind them on my wrists.

"Unarmed as I was, I disdained to suffer this treatment tamely. I seized the partizan which the Count held to my breast, and should soon have wrested it from him, had not his associate come to his assistance, and, drawing his sword, sworn he would plunge it to my heart if I did not desist.

"I found farther resistance ensured my immediate death, and was, at length, obliged to submit. My hands were manacled, and, after being assured that, if I proved tractable, my life would be safe, and I should want for nothing, I was left to meditate on this singular transaction, the iron door being secured, as I could but too well hear, by many locks and bolts.

"During fourteen years confinement, I never saw this fellow afterwards, and have great reason to believe, from what I have been since able to learn, that my brother and the Count made him attend them to the thickest of the forest upon my horse, and there dispatched him and my favourite beast together, as my horse's furniture, my cloak, (which in the heat of the chace I had given to the Count to carry,) and my cutlass, were found at no considerable distance from each other, in the part of the forest which the wolves most infest, who had probably made a meal of this fellow and his horse.

"It was some time before I could sufficiently recollect my scattered senses to survey the apartment in which I was confined. This, however, I at length did. I found it supplied with every conveniency which could contribute to render confinement tolerable.

"Among other things there was a good collection of books, which in such a situation proved a treasure.

"The first idea with which I began the survey of this apartment, was that of escaping. I surveyed it round; but the more I beheld it, the more I was mortified with a conviction of the impossibility of succeeding in any attempt of that kind.

"The windows were very high, and so small, that it would have been impossible to force a man's body through them; though they opened gradually towards the inside of the wall, which was very thick. The chimney was extremely narrow, as was indeed every outlet which was necessary to this chamber of confinement; and it was defended, as I found in an attempt I made to thrust myself up it, by a strong iron grate—perhaps by more than one—nay, if I had made my way to the roof, through the chimney, or had been able to squeeze my body thro' one of the windows, I should scarcely have found myself in a better situation than in my apartment, which was at an immense distance from the ground.

"I found that they had left for me some provisions, a few bottles of wine, and some of water; and, as soon as the melancholy ideas, with which my situation could not fail to impress me, would permit to think of gratifying the calls of nature, I took a slight repast, and throwing myself on the bed, delivered myself to an agitated and broken slumber.

"On the next morning I examined the iron-cased door. To this door you ascended, by some stone steps, from the apartment.

"In returning from this examination, which still contributed to damp my hopes of escape, I found, at the bottom of these steps, another door. It was very strong, made of wood, and furnished with a massy lock and bolts, and in the centre of it was a machine, somewhat similar to those used in convents, which are turned upon a pivot, for the purpose of conveying things from the outside to the persons within.

"While I was musing upon these circumstances, I heard the bolts of the iron door unfastened, and the Count St. Amand entered, armed with more precaution than on the preceding day.

"I upbraided him with his treachery and disloyalty, and approaching, with an intent to seize him, he drew his sword, and swore that my life should answer for any attempt on his person.

"Sir," said he, "if you will submit with patience to your destiny, your confinement shall be rendered as little irksome as possible. You shall want for nothing—but, 'till the period of that confinement, you must not expect to see any person whatever. You shall be allowed pen and ink—and by conveying a note into the box of this inner door, you will make known your wants, which will be supplied."

"So saying, he threw me a key, that I might unlock my fetters, from which I was permitted for the future to be free, and from that moment I saw him no more.

"I was, however, regularly supplied through the medium of this inner door, which he locked and bolted after him, with whatever I wanted, furnished always, as I had reason to believe, by himself in person, though I sometimes suspected, from the difference of the step which I heard, a step with which my ear was not unacquainted, that my brother Astolpho supplied his place.

"I will not detain you with endless projects, and some futile attempts to escape, which always proved abortive, during a period of fourteen years confinement:—Let it suffice to say, that it was at last accomplished in the following singular manner:——

"I was awakened one night by a terrible storm—the wind shook the building to its foundation——the thunder broke in deafening peals over my head—the lightning flashed almost without intermission, so that my prison was perfectly enlightened by its rays.

"I arose from my bed, and paced my chamber, deeply meditating on the awful horrors of the night, when a flash of lightning darted full on the building, attended by a clap of thunder so terrible, that I thought the tottering fabric would have fallen at one blow in ruins to the earth.

"I was struck down, and lay for a short time senseless, and upon recovering myself, was preparing again to lie down on the bed, when, casting my eyes to the other end of the room, I was struck by an object which called all my attention.

"The storm seemed somewhat to have abated, but, as I looked towards the corner of the room, I could perceive the lightning flashing, as I imagined, through the solid wall. I approached the spot—but how can I describe my astonishment, when I perceived the wall to be rent open, by the displacing of several of the stones of which it was composed?

"I removed the rubbish with an eagerness which almost frustrated its own intent, and squeezing my body through the crevice, perceived with a rapture, which I cannot describe, that my escape from my prison was become almost certain, if I would hazard the attempt.

"I fell on my knees on the spot where I stood, and amid the awful horrors of the storm, returned thanks to that Providence whom it had pleased thus, almost miraculously, to relive me from so long and melancholy an imprisonment.

"The lightning (the near approach of which I had so sensibly felt) had fallen on one of the turrets of this old mansion, connected with the apartment in which I was confined, and having torn off the roof, the battlements, and great part of the wall, had left most of the stone staircase within it entire.—When I got through the breach which the storm had made, I found myself on one of the steps of this staircase which now stood, undefended by any wall or ballustrade, winding down on the outside of the building.

"The sight of it was indeed tremendous. The lightning discovered to me the buildings, and the moat beneath, at an immense distance.

"Nothing, perhaps, less than that ardent thirst for liberty, which then possessed me, could have urged me to attempt the descent, ignorant of what steps the storm might have loosened, and what displaced.

"I did not, however, hesitate, but began, boldly, the descent of this awful precipice, for such (narrow, tottering, and undefended, except by part of the wall, which still seemed to cling to the steps here and there) it certainly was.

"After some risque from the looseness of my footing, and the power of the wind, I arrived at last safely at the bottom, and found myself within the mansion.

"Whether, during my confinement, any servants had been kept at this place, or whether the house had been deserted, I do not know. I explored my way through the dark recesses into which the staircase had led me, and after much difficulty, undiscovered by any one, probably because, if there were servants in the house, the storm prevented their hearing me, I found my way out at the door of the hall, and gained the forest, where I passed a night of rapture, unabated by the howling of the storm around me.

"In the morning I made my way to a cottage, whose inmates, little imagining they were protecting their monarch, afforded me shelter and food. They shall not, however, repent their hospitality, if I should be fortunate enough to regain possession of my throne. From this cottage I am come to seek farther shelter with you."

Such was the story which Emanuel related to the prior and the community of St. Julian's—in the course of which it will occur to every one as a singular circumstance, that, instead of subjecting themselves to the hazard of the king's escape from his place of confinement, the conspirators did not immediately take his life.

This was entirely owing to the superstition of Astolpho—a quality which is not infrequently attendant on the most daring courage, tho' seemingly extremely opposite to it in its nature.

Astolpho had been informed, early in life, by an old man who pretended to be deeply versed in judicial astrology, and who was, on that account, much respected by him, that he should not long survive his brother; and this idea, with the truth of which, as with that of all such predictions, he was fully impressed, probably saved Emanuel's life.

He was willing to risque any thing but his own life, which he thought depended on Emanuel's, to obtain the crown.

He might also, perhaps, feel, in the midst of all his ambition, some degree of tenderness towards a relation, who had himself shewn so much affection towards him; and this conjecture is rendered the more probable, when we reflect on his conduct towards the Princess Isabel, whom he has educated with a care and tenderness which, tho' the attachment of the people towards her might perhaps have insured her from any attempt on her life, does not seem to have been necessary from any motives of policy.

During a reign of fourteen years, Astolpho had so well secured himself on the throne of his half-brother, that it was improbable that any sudden irruption in favour of Emanuel should be attended with success.

It became, therefore, necessary that he should be secreted with care, 'till the strength of his friends could be tried; and it was agreed that he should change the garment in which he escaped—which was a plain dress, provided for him by the Count de St. Amand, for the habit of the order, and enroll himself among the fathers of St. Julian. With these brave and faithful companions, then, has he resided for upwards of twelve months, during which time his health, which, notwithstanding his unwearied practice of taking as much exercise every day as the size of his prison would allow, was somewhat impaired, has been re-established, and measures have been most cautiously and indefatigably pursued to restore him to the throne, which his unworthy relation has usurped.

In the course of this pursuit, the young Count Rhinaldo, whose father, Count Roderic, surnamed the Hardy, is lord of the Castle at the foot of the mountain, and of the domain around it, was deemed worthy to be entrusted with this secret and important event.

Virtuous, enterprising, and active, he was called by his father at the conclusion of the last campaign from the bustle of the field, to partake of that retirement to which the displeasure of Astolpho had condemned this formidable leader.

Retirement at such a period of life, and with such a disposition, but ill suited the temper of Rhinaldo. He grew, on a sudden, melancholy, reserved, and gloomy, and his only consolation, amid the despondency which seemed to surround him at the Castle of his father, was the conversation of the fathers of St. Julian.

Knights, like himself, they still delighted in the tales of former times, but their rashness was tempered by experience, and their ferocity by age.

It was in this society that father Anthony, (for so was Emanuel called,) became acquainted with him, and tho' he had been at variance with Count Roderic, who had, at a very early period of life, imbibed some discontent from a conduct which he had thought partial in the king, and had so behaved himself upon the discovery, as totally to alienate the affections of Emanuel, yet that Prince discovered so much virtuous energy and early wisdom in the conduct and conversation of the son, that he became speedily attached to him, and at length ventured to discover to him his secret—but under a solemn engagement, that he would never reveal it to his father, whom he could not prevail upon himself to confide in.

How was the loyalty of Rhinaldo confirmed, when he beheld in Emanuel, the father of his adored Lady Isabel! He pledged his faith to this revered but unfortunate sovereign, and became one, among a very few, entrusted with a plot lately formed in the capital, which has unfortunately proved unsuccessful, to seize upon the palace and the person of Astolpho.

What will be the event of this attempt to re-establish on the throne this brave but injured monarch, it is impossible at present to decide.

His friends are busy in the southern and western parts of the kingdom, and have already raised forces, which appear formidable to Astolpho. At present that usurper has a superiority at the Castle, and has made some vigourous attacks on the mount, which is most resolutely defended by Emanuel and my brethren there, who have again resumed their arms. Old as I am, I had determined to join them; but it was judged that the little service I was able to perform in favour of a cause to which I feel so strong an attachment, might be, with better success, attempted here. I have a frequent but guarded communication with them, which my situation has hitherto concealed from the eyes of the enemy. If, however, it should at length be discovered, I shall remember that I am a knight, and gladly yield up the few hours which yet might have been spared to me in the cause of true loyalty.

The hermit thus concluded his story, which agitated the breast of Count Tancred with mingled indignation, pity, and surprise.

It for a while suspended his sorrows for the Princess Albina, and he felt that he had one more cause to lament the unhappy tardiness of his cure.

CHAP. XVI.

RHINALDO, under the disguise of a servant, became again familiarized to the apartments of his paternal mansion.

He was every day a witness to the increasing favour of Rhodolpho with the usurper, a circumstance which excited less surprise in his breast than grief and indignation. He daily heard Emanuel treated in the Court of Astolpho as an impostor—a slander, to which, indeed, a claim revived after a silence of fourteen years, afforded some foundation; and he was aware that Rhodolpho was probably the only man who could lay open the foulness and falsehood of such an assertion.

He was not, however, aware of one circumstance, which had thrown Astolpho, more completely than he had conjectured, into the hands of his favourite.

The Count St. Amand had, with the paternal fondness which the worst men sometimes feel, entrusted his son, after binding him by many oaths to a strict concealment, with this important secret, as a means by which he might ensure the continuance of Astolpho's favour, in case that Prince should survive the Count—but fortune had done more for him. On the night of Emanuel's escape, he had left behind him, among other things, a book, in which he had minuted every occurrence which he thought worthy of notice during his long confinement.

As every day was much like the preceding one, this work was not very voluminous, but it contained a short account of his arrival at the mansion, and was continued at intervals nearly up to the day of his escape.

Upon visiting the rooms after the escape of the king, the Count St. Amand found this journal, and, even amidst the confusion which seized upon him when he discovered the escape of his prisoner, he did not forget to possess himself of it.

This book, with annotations in many pages of it in his father's hand-writing, all combining to bear testimony to the truth of its contents, fell into the hands of Rhodolpho upon the Count's death; as a did a ring which was known to be Emanuel's, and which, as it was found among the rubbish by the workmen, who repaired the ruins which the storm had made, was probably lost by the king as he forced his way through the aperture in the wall in order to make his escape.

With such proofs in his power, (of the existence of which Astolpho was not ignorant,) it was of the utmost importance to that prince that he should secure to himself the good will of Rhodolpho; and the servile adulation of that young nobleman rendered this by no means a difficult or unpleasant task.

Rhinaldo, however, beheld the influence he was possessed of with the utmost dread, aware as he was that it threw his beloved Isabel compleatly into the power of this unworthy rival. Nor was it long before he was convinced that his fears were but too well founded.

Incessantly employed in endeavours to discover in what part of the Castle the Princess was confined, he in a short time perceived that two of Rhodolpho's servants, who were more constantly than the rest about their master's person at the hours of meals, always attended him with six covers for his table, though he himself always dined and supped with Astolpho; these servants Rhinaldo resolved to watch; and, on the day succeeding that on which he had formed this resolution, he followed them, at the usual hour, towards their lord's apartments—he saw them enter with the covers which had been prepared, and shortly after return, preceded by Rhodolpho, who led them up the great staircase, and unlocking a door, remained at it while they entered a suit of apartments, which Rhinaldo knew to terminate in a spacious chamber, formerly allotted to himself, which extended to the other side of the building. Satisfied with this discovery he returned, and was crossing the court of the castle, to gain the opposite wing, when he was called to his duty, which was on that day to attend at the carrying up Astolpho's dinner.

Mad as he was at the delay which this degrading duty occasioned, he was obliged to submit, and some hours passed before he was at leisure to pursue his intended design, for he could not omit any portion of the servile task allotted to him, without incurring suspicion, which might ruin his design, or without the danger of a dismission, which would effectually frustrate his long-cherished hopes.

Evening had for some time set in, when he found himself at liberty, and a second time crossing the court, gained the side of the house which had been so long the object of his anxious solicitude.—He ascended a staircase, every step of which was familiar to him; though it seemed little frequented by the present inhabitants of the Castle; and had not indeed been much used by his father, as it led to the most ancient part of this extensive pile, a part which had been for many years much neglected, for the more modern portion of the building, on which great cost had been bestowed. The steps of Rhinaldo, however, had frequently traced this venerable and neglected fabric.—He loved to muse in a long gallery, hung with the pictures of his ancestors, and rendered a fit object for the indulgence of that enthusiasm which is often the companion of youthful imagination, by the gloom which the narrow, coloured panes, and massy frames of its gothic windows threw around.

To this gallery, which extended from wing to wing on one side of the building, a space of very considerable length, Rhinaldo now ascended, and tracing his way along it by the light of the moon, arrived at the opposite door to that by which he had entered.—He was much mortified when he found that this door, which was not far distant from the apartment, in which he conjectured that the Lady Isabel was confined, was locked.—He tried in vain to open or force it, and was considering what step he should pursue, when he recollected, that over the gallery there was another room of the same size, which had never been used but as a loft, through which he might pass and gain the apartments; on that side of the castle; he therefore returned along the gallery to the staircase he had just quitted, and ascending still by a more narrow part of it, which, as it had been very seldom frequented, was somewhat incumbered by rubbish, he passed through one or two small rooms and arrived at the door of the loft; this he laid hold on, and pushing it against some rubbish, which for a moment prevented its opening, he entered the loft.

As he entered he heard a noise at the farther end, and, by the light of the moon, imagined he perceived the figure of a man, which starting from a seat, disappeared hastily by the opposite door. He could not, indeed, distinctly ascertain the figure of this object, in delineating which he was, perhaps, deluded by his imagination; but upon the coolest reflexion he was convinced he had seen something move in that end of the loft, and that whatever it might be that was in motion, it was an object so polished as to reflect the moon's beams, and by which alone he had been enabled to discover it.

He puzzled himself in vain for some time, with reflexions on this singular circumstance, till at last, recollecting the primary object of his pursuit, he passed the loft, and enter-

ing at the opposite door, which he found open, descended
by another staircase, and soon arrived at those apartments
from which the door of the gallery below had excluded
him.—He proceeded through two small rooms and gained
a third, which joined to the apartment in which he supposed
the princess to be confined.—This apartment, the last of
those which were inhabited on that side of the house, had
formerly communicated by a small door with the room in
which Rhinaldo now stood; but this door had long been
nailed up, and the door-way had been plaistered over on the
inside, to render it level with the wall, at a time when, by
Count Roderic's order, the apartment had been hung with
an elegant tapestry.—At this door Rhinaldo listened, but
could hear nothing.—He examined the fastenings, they
were old and worn with rust; he found that if he could procure instruments, it would not be difficult to draw the nails,
and thus open the door.—This he determined to attempt
at an hour when the family were asleep, when he had little
doubt that he might work undiscovered in so retired a part
of the mansion.

Having formed this resolution, he returned through the
loft, and mingling with the other servants, occupied himself
in the duties of his office till the hour of rest approached.

A stillness now began by degrees to invade the roar and
tumult to which the hours of wassel gave birth.—Astolpho
and his companions had retired to rest, and the menial servants only waited till some of his inferior officers, who were
indulging themselves in a sober silent debauch, should chuse
to retire.

Rhinaldo, who had taken care to provide himself with
tools fit for his purpose, waited with anxiety for the conclusion of their supper—the clock from the turret tolled out
twelve, and this party, as if awakened from their lethargy
by the sound, arose, to the secret joy of Rhinaldo, who saw
them take their route to their several apartments. He retired

to a small room allotted to him, and waited till the castle was buried in a profound silence; then taking his tools in his hand, he set out in pursuit of his purpose.

As he passed the door of the long gallery, in his way to the loft above it, he heard a noise, and imagining that some part of the family were yet up, he determined to enter the gallery, and wait there.—He had no sooner set his foot within the door-way than he felt himself for a moment rivetted by surprise to the spot where he stood.—The moon shone in full splendor thro' the windows of the gallery, and clad with an awful and solemn beauty, the gothic ornaments of the place; when, by the light it diffused, Rhinaldo beheld, seated on a chair, beneath the picture of his father, the same figure which he had before distinguished in the loft above, and which he could now plainly perceive to be that of a man, in complete armour.

As he entered the room the figure started up, and disappeared by the opposite door, which Rhinaldo had found shut on his previous visit to that place. As soon as he could recover himself from the sudden astonishment and confusion with which he was overwhelmed; he followed hastily along the gallery, but found, when he arrived at the further end of it, the door, by which the figure had disappeared, still locked. This circumstance impressed him with new astonishment, not unmixed, in spite of all the firmness of his mind, with terror; he returned, however, through the gallery, and ascended the other flight of stairs, in order to pass through the loft to the apartment in which he was to proceed to work.

As he entered the loft he again saw the same figure which he had seen twice before, standing in the opposite door-way, and upon the noise he made on entrance it again disappeared.—Rhinaldo now, agitated by a thousand different sensations, rushed hastily forward, and passing swiftly through the loft, gained the staircase at the other end of it, which led to the apartments which he had designed to visit.—He descended the stairs swiftly, and examined minutely every apartment—all was silence—he could perceive no object—he could hear no sound.—After musing some time he begun to be convinced that his imagination had deceived him, and searching for the little door which was to be the object of his labours, he proceeded to work. As he was fearful, if the adjoining apartment should really prove to be that of the Lady Isabel, the noise he might make would alarm her, he proceeded on his work with extreme caution, and nearly an hour had elapsed before he had compleatly conquered all the difficulties which opposed themselves to him, and had opened the door, which he did very gently, lest the creaking of its rusty hinges should be heard.

He now found himself close to the apartment which he meant to explore; the only separation between the two rooms being a thin partition of plaister, which cased the door-way on the inside.—He listened—all was silent; this was to be expected at such an hour. He thrust one of the implements he had with him through the wall, to discover whether there was any light in the room; but the tapestry which covered the walls prevented this discovery.

He paused again.—After a short time he distinctly heard the step of a man in the chamber, and concluding, from this circumstance, that his conjecture, as to this apartment, had been ill-founded, was preparing to retire, when he heard the voice of a man, who, addressing himself to another, in a low but hasty tone, said, "My lord, the King requires your presence immediately."

"Cursed ill-fortune," replied the other, in a voice which he knew to be Rhodolpho's, "What can he want with me at this hour?"

"Something has dreadfully disordered him; he has risen from his bed; his looks are full of perplexity and horror; and he has desired your immediate presence."

They now walked slowly from the place, and Rhinaldo, satisfied that he had taken his trouble for nothing, retired.

CHAP. XVI.

AFTER passing through the two adjacent apartments, Rhinaldo arrived at that door of the gallery which was locked, and was about to ascend the staircase which led to the loft above it, in order to return in his usual way, when he again beheld the same figure on the stairs, leaning with one hand against the wall.—The moon, through a small window, which gave light to this part of the staircase, disclosed, compleatly, the head of this figure; in the countenance of it, Rhinaldo, from the momentary view he gained, (for at this approach the figure turned hastily from him and disappeared) was convinced, that he saw that of his murdered father.—The helmet was his—the plumage, the very plumage he wore when he had last attended him in the field.

Struck with horror at this sight, he felt himself for some moments rooted to the spot where he stood; but recovering himself, at length he ran hastily up the staircase, and entered the lobby.—He could see nothing—he listened—all was still.—In a short time he heard a murmur ascending from below, and the treading of several footsteps, as if the inhabitants of the castle were already stirring.

He crossed the loft, and descending into the hall, found several of Astolpho's attendants, and some of the servants, who were collected in different groupes, and huddled close together, as if listening to some dreadful tale.—He joined one of these parties, and learned, that the cause of the confusion he witnessed was the disordered state of the king, who had been awakened from his sleep in such a paroxysm of horror, as to have spread, by his conduct, a general alarm.

The cause of this was not certainly known, because, as

soon as he became again master of himself, he imputed his alarm to a dream, and ordered his attendants again to their repose; but the first report had been, that the figure of Count Roderic, who was generally suspected to have been slain by his order, had appeared to him compleatly armed; that it had opened his curtains, and presented a dagger to his breast; but had, after a short pause, with a look of mingled contempt and pity, withdrawn it and disappeared. This figure had been seen by none of the attendants in the anti-chamber, who were buried in a profound sleep, except one indeed, who declared that he saw something brush by him, and pass out at the door; but as this person had been in company with the rest, drinking freely in the course of the evening, this was generally imputed to the fumes of the liquor with which he had been indulging himself.

In the hurry of the first alarm Count Rhodolpho had been sent for, but that order had been now countermanded: the king had sent to him, as he had done to others of his attendants, to tell him that he was not wanted, and had shut himself up in his chamber with the captain of his guard, an approved and valiant knight.

Agitated by this fresh intelligence, which concerned him so nearly, and bore so palpable a relation to the appearance which had three times encountered his sight in the course of the same evening, Rhinaldo was lost in meditation—his companions, dropping off one by one, left him alone in the hall; he sat musing for some time; at length, no longer able to bear the accumulated pangs of the various feelings which assailed him, he resolved again to explore that part of the building where he had already beheld this singular spectre; to address it——if it fled, to follow it.—In short, at all events, if possible, to put an end to the horrid suspence which now oppressed him.

He accordingly ascended, for the third time, to the gallery.—All there was still and silent.—He again visited the

loft.—He thought he perceived something—he advanced—
it was only a singular appearance at an angle of the wall,
caused by a particular direction of the moon-beam.—He
passed along the loft, and began to descend by the opposite
staircase.

He had reached the door of those apartments, in one of
which he had so lately been at work, when he heard a noise
behind him, as if on the top of the staircase, near the door of
the loft. He re-ascended five or six steps of the staircase, and
thought he perceived at the top of it something moving.—
He was rushing forward to ascertain it, when he was stopped
by loud and repeated shrieks from below; they were in a
female voice.—The Lady Isabel was ever present to his
imagination. He thought the voice was her's—he listened
for a moment.—His suspicions grew stronger. He leaped
down the stairs; the shrieks were repeated.—He listened—
they led him into the little suite of apartments—he rushed
through them in an instant; in the third was the door which
he had recently opened.—He now heard the voice of his
Isabel distinctly; it proceeded from the apartment which he
had at first supposed to be her's, and from which he was only
separated by a slight partition of plaister.—The shrieks for
a moment ceased.—He heard the voice of Isabel, in a tone
of terror and supplication, imploring the mercy of some
person:

"Alas!" said she, "for pity's sake spare me.—If I must at last
become your wife, cruel as is my destiny, I must submit; but
for heaven's sake—for your own sake, do not attempt a deed
which will call down accumulated vengeance on your own
head."

"I thank you," said Rhodolpho, (for it was to him that this
prayer was addressed) in a tone of cruel and bitter raillery,
"for your consent to marry me, thus unsolicited; while you
were your uncle's presumptive heir, it was something; but
your father's rash attempt has hurl'd you from his favour."

"At least," said Isabel, in a more determined voice; "dread the vengeance of that father! of my uncle!"

"As to your uncle," said Rhodolpho, in a familiar tone; "my dear creature, he will never quarrel with a man for lowering your pride, in the present moment; and as to your father, I never fear dangers at a distance.—Come," he continued, "do not force me to harsh measures."

The shrieks of the Lady Isabel were now repeated. Rhinaldo, in a transport of rage and indignation, setting his back against the slender fence which separated the two apartments, easily broke through it, and lifting the tapestry which covered it, discovered his beloved Isabel, in a night-dress, struggling with Rhodolpho.—He sprung upon him like a lion, and seizing him with both hands by the collar, soon separated him from the princess.

"Vile dishonourable coward," said he, "who bravest distant dangers! shudder at one which has come thus unexpectedly upon thee, in the midst of thy villanies."

"Base-born hind! dost thou know me?" said Rhodolpho.—"Unhand me instantly."

Rhinaldo still held him; but perceiving that he felt about his girdle with his right-hand, he seized it just as it had grasped a dagger, and wrenching the weapon from him, bade him prepare to die. A shriek from the Lady Isabel now awakened his attention; and, throwing the dagger from him, he flew towards her, and conducted her, almost fainting, to a chair.

The apartment they were now in had been assigned to the Lady Isabel, and was used by her as her dressing-room. On one side of it was a small apartment, in which stood her bed, connected with it, by an arched doorway, over which hung a curtain of silk, which was seldom let down, as it interrupted the free passage of the air.

Rhodolpho, to whose custody her uncle had consigned her, kept the keys of her prison, the outer apartments of which he kept safely locked; and Isabel, relying upon their being secured, neglected to take any precaution with the inner ones, as much, because she thought it useless, as because, by leaving them unfastened she preserved a communication with the chambers of her cousin Ellenor, and her servant Barbara, who were placed in other apartments, nearly adjacent to her's.

Ellenor, who had been awakened by the shrieks of her cousin, flew, with Barbara, to the door of her chamber, and, finding it lock'd, knock'd loud for admittance. Rhinaldo ordered Rhodolpho to admit them, which the other did not chuse to refuse, but opening the door, suffered them to enter, and quitted the apartment.

Ellenor flew to embrace her cousin, and anxiously inquired into the cause of her alarm.—Isabel satisfied her, and expressed the highest sense of the obligation, under which the sudden and mysterious presence and interposition of the stranger had laid her.

"Do you not, then, know me?" said Rhinaldo, falling at her feet, and pressing one of her hands to his lips.

The voice of Rhinaldo, now, for the first time, struck her ears; and the lamp, which burnt in her chamber, gave sufficient light to enable her to distinguish his countenance.

"Rhinaldo," said she, in a voice scarcely audible; she sunk into his arms; and the moments flew, while these lovers gave themselves up to those chaste and pure raptures, which true passion alone can yield, and which the presence of Ellenor, far from restraining, emboldened the lovely Isabel to acknowledge with less reserve.

Raptures like these were not destined to endure long.— Barbara first alarmed them with the intelligence, that she heard the sound of footsteps approaching the chamber; and Rhinaldo instinctively flew to the door, and secured it.

"Oh Rhinaldo!" exclaimed Isabel, "I know not how you came hither; but, for heaven's sake, if there is any mode of escape, fly from a fate, which, if you should be taken, must doubly embitter the remaining moments of a life, already sufficiently miserable." Here she burst into tears.

Rhinaldo, in a tone of fixed resolution, declared that he would remain where he was, to protect Isabel and her cousin; but this resolution was combated with tears and intreaties by Ellenor, as well as Isabel, who represented to him, that after the alarm which had been given, it was impossible that any immediate danger could accrue to Isabel; and, that as to any future evil, it was only by keeping himself free from discovery, that he could entertain a hope of averting it.

"Fly, then," said Isabel, the tears streaming from her lovely eyes; "at least for my sake."

This argument was, with Rhinaldo, unanswerable.— They now distinctly heard many footsteps in the adjacent chamber.—He embraced Isabel and her cousin, and hastily quitted the apartment by the cavity through which he had entered it.

CHAP. XVII.

RHINALDO, who did not doubt but that in a few minutes his mode of retreat would be discovered, fastened the little door after him, by the bolts which still remained unimpaired, and hesitated for a moment what step to take. He conjectured that Rhodolpho might not have discovered him, and thought that no place offered more security than his own chamber, if he could gain it unperceived.

He heard the voices of several men in Isabel's apartment, and had no longer time to hesitate. He moved quickly up the stairs, and crossing hastily thro' the loft, began to descend on the other side. He had already passed the gallery door, when he heard voices at the foot of the stairs, and was enabled to distinguish, among others, these words: "Here is the staircase which leads to that side of the house."

He returned in a moment, and ascended again to the loft.

The gallery door was open, and he judged that his pursuers would take that way, which would compel them to return, and that he should thus gain time. They indeed entered the gallery; but instead of returning, upon finding the door shut, they forced it open; and when Rhinaldo, who had in the mean time crossed the loft, prepared to descend, he heard their voices at the bottom of the staircase. In the utmost perplexity, he looked anxiously and eagerly around him, for an outlet; the door of the loft, on this side, opened into a small square room, which formed a kind of landing-place, whence the stairs descended. In one corner of this landing-place was a small door which opened, as Rhinaldo discovered, on a narrow winding staircase, leading, as it seemed, to the roof of the castle. As he had no time for choice, he began to ascend; but was suddenly surprised by a noise above him, on the staircase, he listened, and thought he heard the steps of a man. Astonished as he was, he continued to ascend, feeling his way along the wall with his hand, which at last encountered a small door; he pushed against it—it opened; but was immediately closed by some person from the inside, and fastened.

Thus excluded, he was obliged to pursue his way up the staircase; it ended in a narrow room, in the ceiling of which was a trap-door; but there was no ladder to enable him to reach it.—He heard a trampling in the room below. He looked round, and discovered a small window, the casement of which was almost entirely gone.—It looked out upon the battlements, he perceived that it was just wide enough to admit the passage of his body through it.—He caught hold of a bar, which divided it in two, and springing up, thrust himself, with some little difficulty, through it, and found himself on the battlements of the loftiest part of the castle.—He pursued his way along them, though he found it somewhat impeded by the ruins which had fallen from the tower above him, out of which he had escaped, which was the most ancient part of the whole edifice, and, as has been before observed, the most neglected.

He arrived at length at a door, leading into one of the turrets, with which these battlements were flanked; this turret was nearly in as ruinous a state as the tower above. And Rhinaldo, when he pushed open the door, found himself impeded by the rubbish which had fallen on the inside of it.—He entered, however, with some little difficulty, and found himself at the top of the winding staircase of the turret, by which he resolved to descend; it was very old and broken; the walls emitted unusual dampness; and it bore every mark of having been deserted for ages.—After pursuing this descent for a considerable time, he found himself at a kind of resting-place; this was a long narrow vaulted passage, branching off to the left of the staircase, which, however, still continued to descend.

Rhinaldo felt his way along this passage, which, from the length of time he had already been descending, and from its arched form, he judged to be situated among the vaults under the castle, and having pursued it for some time, found, at the end of it, a low door, seemingly very strong, studded with large nails, and almost choked up with rubbish.—He now returned towards the staircase of the turret—he listened, but could hear nothing of his pursuers, who, it was probable, had given up their search.—He hesitated whether he should return or no; but curiosity prompting him, he resolved to explore to what profounder depth the staircase extended, having already conducted him, as he was convinced, many feet underground.

He began again to descend—the staircase continued, winding downwards, till it ended in a low arched passage, extending in a contrary direction to that above.—The mouth of this passage was closed by an iron grate, which hung sloping towards the ground, supported only by one of the hinges, (the other having given way) and the bolt on the opposite side. This grate Rhinaldo easily threw to the ground, and entered the passage.

After having walked for a considerable time, and immured in a total darkness, and gradually descending as he went; he thought of returning; but perceiving, suddenly, that he began to ascend, he resolved again to proceed, and finding himself impelled by a curiosity, which every moment interested him more and more; he continued to move forward, feeling his way with his hands, and gradually ascending, till his foot struck against something, which, upon examination, he found to be a stone step; he felt with his hands, and discovered that he was at the bottom of a staircase, which he began to ascend.

This staircase was of considerable length, and Rhinaldo, who felt himself incommoded by the damp air of the subterraneous vault, was compelled, after some time, to stop and rest himself.

After a pause, he again proceeded, and found himself at length at the summit of the staircase, his farther progress being opposed by a trap-door of great weight. Rhinaldo placed his back against this door, and after some vigourous attempts, he succeeded in raising it.—As it rose he felt himself almost covered with rubbish, and found, by a noise above, something had been displaced by his efforts.—He entered a place, damp, close, and confined; he could not conjecture what it might be.—As he walked cautiously round it, he felt his progress impeded; he stooped to discover the cause of this impediment, and his hand alighted on a coffin, covered with velvet, and studded thick with nails.

Wrapt in the reflexions which this singular object gave rise to, he proceeded slowly, till he came to a flight of steps, which he ascended, and found, at the top of them, a pair of folding doors.—These he attempted to open, but, for a long time, in vain; at length, old, rotten, and crazy, they yielded to the vigourous and repeated efforts, which the horror he conceived at being buried alive urged him to make, and he found himself within the iron railing which surrounded a magnificent tomb, in a small chapel, within that belonging to the monastery of St. Julian. This place he knew (for the moon still shed her mellow light through the painted windows of the chapel) to be the tomb of his ancestors; a privileged place of burial for the lords of the castle, and domain around.

His rapture on this discovery is scarcely to be conceived.— He saw the usurper, Astolpho, delivered into the hands of his gracious and rightful sovereign, the great and good Emanuel. He saw his father revenged, and his princess delivered!

After having opened a gate in the iron railing surrounding the tomb, which he effected by putting his hand between the bars, and pushing back a bolt; he passed through a wicket of the same materials, which separated the little chapel from that of the convent, and entered the latter; but despairing of making himself heard before the chapel should be opened at mattins, he placed himself on a bench in the choir, and musing on the singular adventures of the evening, was at length overtaken by sleep.

He had slept but a short space of time, when he was awakened by the step of some person walking slowly down the aisle, in which he sat.—What were his emotions, when he beheld, advancing towards him, the same armed figure which he had thrice before discovered in the course of the same evening!

He was a second time convinced that it was the armour of his father; the vizor of the helmet was up; he could no longer doubt it; the eye of his father was bent full upon him.—Rhinaldo fell on his knee, and with a mixture of enthusiastic affection and reverential awe exclaimed:

"O sacred shade! which bearest the form of the most honoured, the most revered of fathers, disclose, I conjure thee, the cause of this most solemn visitation."

"Can it be Rhinaldo!" exclaimed the seeming spectre, in

the voice of Count Roderic; "arise, my son, and tell how it happens that I thus encounter thee."

These words almost bereft Rhinaldo of his senses.—The surprise of the moment was scarcely to be borne.—That the father he supposed murdered should thus unaccountably stand before him! He seemed growing to the pavement, where he kneeled.—His father saw the conflict, and, advancing, raised him from the ground, and embraced him tenderly. Rhinaldo now recovered himself.—He fell again at the feet of his father, and seizing his mailed hand, pressed the cold rivets to his lips, and bedewed it with the tears of filial affection.

A third person now joined them, who proved to be a faithful domestic of Count Roderic, named Hugo; and some time was spent, between the father and son, in expressing their mutual surprise at so unexpected a meeting.

Rhinaldo having seated himself by his father, gave him an account of all the circumstances which had, on his side, conduced to so extraordinary an event; and when he had finished his story, his father gratified his curiosity, by a short relation of the circumstances which had, on his part, contributed to this singular encounter.

He told him, that upon perceiving Astolpho's intentions, which, though he had suspected them, he did not find himself enabled to resist, confirmed by his conduct when he entered the castle; he had, himself, firmly determined not to quit it, but to lie concealed till some opportunity should offer itself of regaining his lawful possession, or at least of executing vengeance on his enemies. That in order to effect this, he had recourse to the advice and assistance of his noble and valued friend, Leopold, who had agreed to leave the castle, and join the forces of Emanuel (though he had not yet declared himself on his side) on the western frontiers, clad in a suit of Count Roderic's armour, and accompanied by a chosen party of brave friends, who were themselves, that the deception might be more certain, to be persuaded that it was Roderic that accompanied them.

This scheme succeeded but too well for Leopold, who, being taken for his friend, was pursued by the malignant hatred of Astolpho, and perished.——Count Roderic in the mean time remained secreted in the old part of the castle, confining himself in the day time to a small room, which opened on the staircase, leading to the tower, from the battlements below which Rhinaldo had escaped.

He was here supplied with necessaries by the means of his faithful domestic, Hugo, who mixed, unsuspected, with the servants of the castle.—From him he learned the death of his friend, and, in a transport of grief and indignation, formed a firm resolution to revenge it. He resolved, however, to delay the execution of his vengeance till the time when other circumstances should determine him to leave the castle. Since the period in which the conduct of Astolpho had become, towards him, that of an implacable enemy, Roderic, whom, after many years of faithful service, not even the juster claims of Emanuel would have induced to appear in arms against the usurper, suffered overtures to be conveyed, through the means of Hugo, to his oppressed and virtuous prince; through the same channel he received information, that a company of men at arms would quarter, on the very evening when this eventful meeting took place, at about five miles from the castle.—Count Roderic resolved to join them; but before he executed that resolve, he determined to exact the vengeance he meditated for the murder of his friend. Hugo had bribed the centinel on the bridge, that they might be suffered to pass at a more early hour than usual. Two of the Count's horses were ready in the stable; and it was highly probable, that an officer of the Count's appearance, though he would scarcely have been permitted to enter them, might be suffered to quit the lines unsuspected.

This would probably have been the case, had he pursued only his design of escaping; but his mind was agitated by the hopes of approaching vengeance. He was armed by the assistance of Hugo, and waited with impatience for the hour when the centinel on the bridge should be relieved, that the man whom Hugo had bribed might take his turn; it was during this period of suspense, that he was thrice seen by Rhinaldo.

At length the hour approached; he descended to the chamber where he knew Astolpho slept.—He passed the anti-chamber with caution; the officers were buried in a profound sleep; he approached the bed of Astolpho, and putting aside the curtains, drew his dagger.—Astolpho awaked, and fixed his opening eyes on him till they exhibited a degree of horror, which, in some measure, recalled Count Roderic to himself. The usurper lay speechless, under the impression of the most agonizing terrors.

Roderic was unfit for the office of an assassin.—He was a knight of hitherto unstained reputation; the victim before him he had long obeyed as his sovereign.—He sheathed his dagger, and slowly quitted the room, leaving Astolpho, who was extremely superstitious, under a firm conviction, that the object he had beheld was the spirit of the murdered Roderic, who had appeared to reproach him with his guilt.

The Count retired, as he had entered, unmolested; and his next object was to effect his retreat from the castle. He returned to the chamber in the staircase, in search of Hugo.—The castle was now alarmed, and it became necessary to wait till all should again become quiet.

In the course of a short period the search after Rhinaldo commenced, and led his pursuers to the very part of the castle in which the Count was concealed. When he heard their footsteps he did not, for a moment, doubt that he was the object of their search.—He heard them at the bottom of the staircase, the room in which Count Roderic was concealed, which was in the tower, communicated by a flight of narrow stairs with the platform.—There was no time for hesitation.—The Count, accompanied by Hugo, ascended, and they found themselves on the loftiest part of the roof of the castle; but even here, if pursued, they must be taken.

There seemed no mode of escape, unless they could gain the battlements below.—They perceived, on examination, that part of the parapet had in one place fallen in, towards the battlements, and rendered the descent not very difficult; they resolved to attempt it, and succeeded.

They pursued the path which Rhinaldo had trod before them; it was, indeed, the only one they could take; they came to the turret—it promised to them an asylum, as it had done to him before; they entered it; the courage of Count Roderic was as little to be daunted by the prospect of the subterraneous passage as that of his son, and the necessity of attempting his escape was, perhaps, more urgent.

He entered it, accompanied by Hugo, unconscious whither it might lead him; for it had been long before his time disused, and the very knowledge of it, though palpably formed to add strength to the castle, by affording a communication with the mount, buried in oblivion.—They arrived in the chapel at the period when Rhinaldo's fatigues had buried him in that sleep from which the sound of his father's footsteps awakened him.

CHAP. XVIII.

DAY had scarcely begun to encroach upon the pale light which the moon had diffused over the venerable walls of the chapel, when the sacristan unbarred the door, and was surprised by the sight of Count Roderic and his son. He conducted them, at their desire, to the officer of the guard, in whom Rhinaldo immediately discovered his friend Anselmo. After mutual embraces Rhinaldo informed him of the singular adventures which had led his father and himself to that spot; and Anselmo introduced them to the presence of Emanuel, who had already arisen, and was in arms.—This gracious prince received Rhinaldo with a cordial embrace; for he had witnessed the virtues of this young knight, during their intimacy, while he concealed the rank, under the garb and name of Father Anthony.—To Count Roderic his demeanour was cordial, frank and open.

He had, not long before he was dispossessed of his throne, by the perfidy of Astolpho, conceived some displeasure at the conduct of Roderic, whose fiery unbending spirit had compelled the king at length to banish him his presence, and the intelligence he received, upon his enlargement, that this nobleman had, for many years, possessed, in a very high degree, the favour and confidence of Astolpho, led him to suspect that he was privy to the perfidy which had deprived him of his liberty and his crown. This suspicion, unfounded, as in truth it was; for Roderic owed his rise in the court of Astolpho, to his recent disgrace with Emanuel; and his continuance in the confidence of that usurper, to his power in the state, and his conduct in the field, so firmly possessed the mind of Emanuel, that though he had learned his late disgrace at the court of Astolpho, he did not think it safe to trust him with the secret, on which, not only his hopes of again ascending the throne of Lombardy, but even his very life depended. These suspicions were now wiped away; his displeasure had long subsided, and the daring spirit, and undisguised open temper and demeanour, which had procured this nobleman the appellation of Roderic the Hardy, again obtained their former credit in the mind of Emanuel.

The discovery of the subterraneous passage was made known to the king, and after a council of the knights had been called, it was agreed, that the castle should be surprised by the means of this inlet, while every preparation was made for an active and vigorous cooperation from without.

The rising sun had not long shed its golden light on the turrets of Count Roderic's Castle, before a knight, completely armed, arrived at the gate and demanded admission to the presence of Astolpho. As soon as that prince had arisen, and a counsel had been summoned, he was admitted. This knight, who was of a figure in which strength, grace, and agility were combined, was magnificently armed, and a large sable plume waved on his helmet.—He advanced towards the chair in which Astolpho was seated, and bending one knee to the ground, demanded justice against a knight of his train, whom he pledged himself to prove a recreant, false to his God, and to his king; an oppressor, and base wrong-doer, towards that sex which he was bound by his oath, and the order he profaned, to succour and protect.

Astolpho promised him the battle, and demanded if the knight were in presence, urging him, at the same time, to speak boldly, and of good heart.—The knight with the sable plume then rising, lifted the vizor of his helmet, and discovered the face of Count Tancred. He fixed his eyes on Rhodolpho, who stood near the chair of the king, and addressed him thus:

"Count Rhodolpho, as thou art a knight, attend.—Thou holdest in a rigorous and cruel captivity, if thy savage rage hath not yet destroyed her, the Princess Aspasia, the sister of this injured monarch, whose favour thou abusest.—The truth of this I pledge myself to make good upon thy head, when, and at what weapons, (provided they be such as may become a knight) thou wilt."

At these words Count Tancred threw down his gauntlet, which Rhodolpho took up, denying, with many asseverations, but with manifest confusion, the truth of the charge.

Astolpho, in whose countenance, amidst the strongest marks of astonishment, a thousand passions seemed struggling for mastery, arose, and ordering the lists to be prepared, and the battle to take place on the succeeding morning, at day-break, left the chamber, and the council broke up.—In the mean time, Count Tancred, who was known to many of the knights in Astolpho's train, was welcomed to the castle, and care was taken that he should be honourably treated till the next morning should arrive.

Astolpho, in the mean time, remained involved in the deepest perplexity. Among his many faults, want of affection towards this sister had no place. He was fond of her, and it was much against his inclination that he had felt himself compelled to sacrifice her to the arms of the Count St. Amand.—His indignation, therefore, against Rhodolpho was raised to the highest pitch, by the very idea, that the accusation of Count Tancred might be true; but the important secret, of which this favourite was master, compelled him to stifle his resentment and to hide in smiles the rage which rankled in his heart; for he well knew, that many persons of the first consequence, who at present supported his cause, did it from a conviction, which had been artfully instilled into them, that his opponent was an impostor, and that Emanuel had actually perished, as had been reported.

While he was musing in his chamber, agitated by these reflections, he was surprised by the presence of Rhodolpho, who had the privilege of entering this apartment.——He could not readily account for this visit, at such a season, and was not a little surprised to find, that the cause of it was the anxious desire which Rhodolpho felt to make a solemn denial of the foul charge, preferred against him in the presence of his sovereign, a charge which he solemnly averred to be founded in the most atrocious falshood, and the most inveterate malignity, which, he added, he did not doubt he should fully prove on the succeeding morning; protesting at the same time, with the strongest asseverations, that he had not seen the Countess since the death of his father.

This declaration was graciously received by Astolpho,

and was, indeed, highly grateful to him.—He was willing to believe it true; but in spite of his inclination, he felt some doubts which he could not wholly suppress. He had long suspected the courage of Rhodolpho, and could scarcely account for his meeting this charge with such determined resolution. This resolution, however, if it was not a proof that he was innocent, was, at least, a strong one that he was willing to appear so; a circumstance which was calculated to spare to Astolpho much mortifying self-humiliation; nor could he help looking with some secret anxiety towards the event of the battle, which, by the death of Rhodolpho, might free him from a subject already become too powerful not to cause him much uneasiness.

CHAP. XIX.

R HODOLPHO, in the mean time, who had never made this declaration till he had taken a resolution effectually to prevent the discovery of its falshood, thought of nothing less than meeting Count Tancred in the field.—His brain, fertile in every project of villany, had engendered the plan of preventing the combat, before he had pledged himself to Astolpho, that he would so ardently embrace that method of proving his innocence, and he retired from that prince's chamber to give more maturity to his design.—He knew no method of preventing the combat, which was to take place in the morning, so effectual as that of assassinating his adversary over night; nor did his heart, at once treacherous, cowardly and cruel, revolt at a crime, not sanctioned indeed, but unhappily rendered too frequent by the barbarous manners of the age.

He thought, that by the means of some worthless instruments, about his person, he might be enabled to do this undiscovered; but, at all events, should suspicions arise, he was sure of protection from Astolpho. His only subject of debate now was how to accomplish his infamous design; and after some time spent in deliberation, he formed the following plan:

In consequence of his brutal and unmannerly attack on the defenceless Isabel, during the preceding night that lady had sent a most earnest intreaty to Rhodolpho, that if she was in future to be confined, her place of confinement might be near to his apartments; nor did Rhodolpho, whom the sudden appearance, and mysterious escape of Rhinaldo had filled with strange suspicions and fears, oppose this request; in consequence of which the princess, together with her cousin and attendant, was removed to an apartment nearly adjoining to that of Astolpho.

Rhodolpho, who had the superintendance of the household, though he could not, in this case, act officially, easily procured it to be intimated to the steward, who supplied his place, that the apartment lately quitted by the princess, would afford the most proper accommodation for the strange knight; and that apartment was, upon this intimation, prepared for him.

Rhodolpho now saw his enemy in his hands; he had, in the pursuit of Rhinaldo, discovered the door by which he had escaped; an inlet to the apartment which would be effectually concealed from the unsuspecting inhabitant by the tapestry. Through this door he determined to gave entrance, at midnight, to the ruffian, who had been privy to his infamous design on the Lady Isabel, and to two others of his train, whom this man pointed out as proper instruments for the business.—These miscreants were to dispatch the unfortunate Count and his attendant with their daggers, while Rhodolpho, himself, waited without to assist them in disposing of their bodies.

The plan being thus projected, and the horrid instruments of his infamous design well instructed; he saw his unsuspecting adversary retire from a slight meal, of which he partook with some friends, towards his apartment, for the night.—Astolpho also retired to rest. The tumult of the hall began, by degrees, to subside; and all grew silent.

Rhodolpho alone, with a mind agitated by all the accumulated horrors which fasten on a design so diabolical; yet urged by desperate cowardice to the perpetration of his guilt, paced, with trembling step, the still gloomy recesses of the castle.—The darkness and silence of the scene shed a double portion of terror, over his mind.

The clock toll'd two—this was the hour at which his accomplices had agreed to meet him—all was still silent, not a step to be heard; he thought they had mistaken the place of appointment, and were, perhaps, already arrived at the spot, which was to be the scene of their infamous action.— He went up stairs, passed through the gallery, and arrived at the little door; he found no person there; the door was still fastened.—He had just opened it, when he heard the footsteps of some persons descending the stairs, on that side of the gallery; they entered the apartment with cautious silent steps.—Rhodolpho advanced towards them:

"Come," said he, in a low tremulous voice; "you are late; the door is opened; be careful, but be resolute. When the deed is done bring the bodies into this room, with every thing that can lead to a discovery, and we will dispose of them."

He had scarcely uttered these words, when he received the sword of the person he addressed through his body, and the voice of Rhinaldo exclaimed, "Die, most infamous assassin."

Rhinaldo, with his father, and friend Anselmo, had been deputed to conduct a select body of Emanuel's troops thro' the subterraneous passage, and they had gained the tower, undiscovered, at the hour when it was judged that the inhabitants of the castle were lulled in profound repose.

Rhinaldo, to whom the safety and protection of the Lady Isabel had been particularly intrusted by her father, hastened, accompanied by a few friends, towards that door, which he knew communicated with her apartment, when he was thus met, and thus accosted by Rhodolpho.

Rhodolpho, when he received the wound, groaned and fell.

Rhinaldo, impressed by the words of Rhodolpho, with the utmost horror, drew his sword from the body, and rushing towards the door, which he found open, entered the apartment, accompanied by his attendants.—On lifting the tapestry, he was surprised to discover, by a light which burned in the room, a person busily employed in arranging and adjusting several pieces of armour; nor was this person, who was Count Tancred's former deliverer, less surprised to see a figure, with a sword imbrued with blood, advance from behind the tapestry.—He dropped the helmet which he held in his hand, and his sudden exclamations awakened his master, Count Tancred, who, slipping on a loose robe, and snatching up a sword which lay by him, entered from his chamber.

The mutual surprise of Rhinaldo and the Count, at this meeting, kept them, for some moments, silent.——Rhinaldo at length informed his friend, in a few words, of the operations of the night, and left him in the care of two of his attendants, while he himself proceeded in search of Isabel.

He passed hastily through the hall, where he already perceived that the business was begun.—A party, near the steps of the range of apartments, which were occupied by Astolpho, boldly, but unsuccessfully opposed another, at the head of which Rhinaldo discovered the plume of his father; he rushed forward to join him; the opposite party retreated up the steps towards the chamber of Astolpho. When they arrived at his chamber, they found it empty; nor were they long in discovering the fate of this guilty and unfortunate Prince.

The vision, as he thought it, of the preceding night, had so much occupied his mind, that the idea of it had, since its appearance, almost incessantly haunted his imagination.

He was observed to be thoughtful and gloomy during the course of the day, and when, after supper, he again retired to bed, he endeavoured in vain to compose himself to rest. After some hours spent in anxiety and terror, he arose, and, dressing himself, walked about his chamber, waiting impatiently for the dawn.

Tired, at length, with his own thoughts, he walked into his anti-chamber, where he found the officers of his guard and other attendants more alert than usual from the alarm of the preceding evening. He conversed with them at intervals for some time. During a pause in the conversation, he thought he heard the sound of footsteps without. The state of his mind made him awake to every suspicion—he listened again—it was no longer to be doubted. In a fit of desperation he rushed out at the head of his few attendants, and met his fate at the very first onset. He was found soon afterwards in the hall covered with wounds, and deprived of every symptom of animation.

After having assisted to beat back the party, who opposed his father, Rhinaldo, whose thoughts were continually bent upon his Isabel, again detached himself with a small party in pursuit of her. From the door of a chamber near to Astolpho's, he saw three females rush forth in all the wildness of sudden and extreme terror.—He met them, and repeating the name of Isabel, stopped their progress.—The first of these females pronouncing the name of Rhinaldo, rushed, as if for protection, into his arms.

It was the Lady Isabel. He conducted her, with her Cousin and attendant, to the apartment of Count Tancred, under whose protection he left them, that he might again join his father; but he found his presence useless. Emanuel had on the preceding day contrived to send intelligence to the party of cavalry which Count Roderic had prepared himself to join, of the plan in agitation, with orders to march in the night, and surprise, if possible, that part of Astolpho's lines, which was opposite to their quarters; at the same time he quitted the priory, and at the head of the chosen troops made an attack on those posts which were the nearest to him. Assaulted at once on opposite sides, and this in the middle of the night, Astolpho's troops made but a feeble resistance, and after a short stand they began to give way on all sides.

Count Roderic, in the mean time, having filled the Castle with his followers, and secured the soldiers within, who, lulled in a fatal security, were most of them surprised without arms, had by this measure effectually disconcerted the troops, who fled before Emanuel; for when they retreated for refuge to the Castle, they found the drawbridge in possession of their enemies.

They threw down their arms—the gates were soon opened to Emanuel, and the dawn of day saw his standard displayed on the walls.

CHAP. XX.

R HINALDO had no sooner saluted his beloved and revered sovereign, and joined in the general congratulations on this singular success, than he flew to the apartment of Count Tancred, that he might introduce his Isabel to a parent whom she had not seen since the age of childhood, and whom she had so long lamented as dead.

He found the chamber empty—but, listening, was attracted by the sound of voices to the little room behind the tapestry, where he discovered the Count, the Lady Isabel, Ellenor, and their attendants.

They were surrounding a wretched man, who seemed mortally wounded. He was sitting on the ground with his back against the wall, and was supported on one side by one of the attendants.

It was Count Rhodolpho, whose groans had led them from the inner chamber to the spot where he lay.—When Rhinaldo entered, he was imploring the pardon of the surrounding audience, but particularly of Tancred, for the offences he had committed, and for the farther ones which he had meditated against them.

He told Count Tancred that the Princess Aspasia was confined in his Castle, and, drawing a ring from his finger, informed him, that upon producing that token to his steward, who had then the command of the Castle, she would be immediately delivered to him.

He confessed, with much contrition, that a passion he had conceived for that lady, stronger than that which bound him towards the Lady Isabel, had caused him thus to secrete her.

As he was much exhausted, Rhinaldo ordered him to be conveyed to the bed in the adjoining chamber.—This was with some difficulty done.—His wound was there dressed, but he died in the course of the succeeding day.

Emanuel, thus restored to his throne, bestowed every day fresh marks of his favour on Rhinaldo and his father, who had been the instruments of this happy revolution.

For Rhinaldo he had long felt and long professed the affection of a father; he no sooner received his long-lost daughter from his hands, than he returned her to this affectionate lover, as the brightest boon he could bestow.—That she was indeed so, ever hour which this enviable father spent in her company convinced him; and, perhaps, if he had not so suddenly given her to Rhinaldo, the difficulty he felt in parting with her might have inclined him to hesitate.

Anselmo now interceded with Rhinaldo to mention his pretensions to the Lady Ellenor; nor were they for a moment disregarded. Emanuel expressed himself happy to be enabled thus to reward the attachment of this deserving young nobleman.

The last words of the miserable Rhodolpho filled the bosom of Count Tancred with a tumult of hopes and fears. He had no sooner been introduced by his friend Rhinaldo to Emanuel, than he prepared to depart for Rhodolpho's Castle, having obtained, in addition to the token he had received, a mandate from the king. It will be needless to describe the rapture which attended the meeting of these lovers.

By the intercession of Rhinaldo the Princess obtained the restoration of the estates of the Count St. Amand, which had been forfeited; and after some time passed in widowhood, from respect to the memory of an husband, who had so little deserved it, she rewarded the faithful attachment of Count Tancred with her hand.

The steady and zealous services of Rugiero were not forgotten by Rhinaldo, who obtained for him an honourable and lucrative situation. Nor did the Lady Isabel overlook in Barbara, the companion of her toils and her dangers; and they found, when, after a reign of many prosperous years, the death of Emanuel exalted them to the throne of Lombardy, in these steady and zealous adherents, true and loyal subjects, and firm and faithful friends.

The hours of adversity which Emanuel had known, had strengthened his mind, which his tedious solitude had much inured to habits of reflection; nor could he fail to observe, as often as he contemplated the combination of circumstances which had brought about a revolution so singular, how seldom, if we would wait patiently for events, we should have reason to inveigh against the success, even in this life, attending criminal actions; and with how little constancy and foresight we continue to lament those circumstances as evil, which eventually, though inexplicably, produce our greatest good.

FINIS.